BUCHANAN'S REVENGE

*Also by Jonas Ward
in Large Print:*

Buchanan Gets Mad
The Name's Buchanan

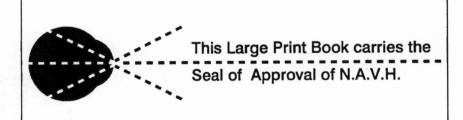

This Large Print Book carries the
Seal of Approval of N.A.V.H.

BUCHANAN'S REVENGE

JONAS WARD

G.K. Hall & Co.
Thorndike, Maine

Published in 1996 by arrangement with Golden West Literary Agency.

G.K. Hall Large Print Western Collection.

The text of this Large Print edition is unabridged.
Other aspects of the book may vary from the original edition.

Set in 16 pt. Bookman Old Style.

Printed in the United States on permanent paper.

Library of Congress Cataloging in Publication Data

Ward, Jonas, 1939–
   Buchanan's revenge / Jonas Ward.
      p.   cm.
   ISBN 0-7838-1877-7 (lg. print : hc)
   1. Buchanan, Tom (Fictitious character) — Fiction.
2. Large type books. I. Title.
[PS3557.A715B84   1996]
813'.54—dc20   96-24242

BUCHANAN'S

REVENGE

ONE

Here's to you, partner," Rig Bogan told Buchanan with a glass raised high, "and here's to me! Who's gonna stop us now?"

Buchanan grinned back at the shorter man, touched the other's glass with his own. "We're hell on wheels," he admitted.

"There is only one sure way to success," put in a third voice, an older voice, with a nasal Eastern sound that contrasted sharply with the soft Texan drawl of the other two. "Hard work," Banker Penney said. "Honest work." His reproving glance lifted to the pair of eagerly poised whiskies. "Sobriety," the banker added.

"Damn well told," Rig Bogan said sincerely and drained the glass, set it down smartly atop the bar and refilled it from the just-opened bottle. "Here's to you, partner," he said to Buchanan again, his freckled, devil-may-care young face aglow with an irrepressible, contagious joy. "And here's to the Double-B Fast Freight! We deliver the goods, by damn if we don't!"

Banker Penney cleared his throat noisily.

7

"I am confident," he said, "that the Double-B Fast Freight will safely and economically deliver all of the shipments consigned to its care. But unless you have received a contract since we entered this foul-smelling saloon . . ."

"Hell's bells, Mr. Penney," Bogan protested, "we just took delivery on the damn wagon five minutes ago . . ."

"For which I paid out three thousand and three hundred dollars in hard cash, young man," the banker snapped back.

"*Two* thousand three hundred," Bogan countered. "Me and Buchanan got a thousand of our own invested in this business."

"Your note is for the amount I stated," Penney said. "It includes the six mules, a year's rent on the freight yard, interest and — ah — other risks connected with any new venture."

Tom Buchanan had been listening to this byplay with an expression of quiet neutrality on his rugged, battle-scarred face. Now he shifted his massive frame, getting the banker's attention, and gazed down at the man out of eyes that were uncommonly blue, deceptively tranquil.

"We know what we owe you," Buchanan said.

"Just so you do," the banker answered, unable to keep a nervous tremor out of his voice whenever the occasion arose to speak

8

directly to this soft-spoken giant.

"And much obliged for the loan, too," Buchanan said.

Mr. Penney blinked. He seemed overwhelmed by the simple gratitude. "Glad to've been able to help," he murmured, then let his pinched face break into one of its rare, fleeting smiles. "You look at me, Mr. Buchanan, like one of the few sound risks I've found since I opened my little bank here in San Antonio."

"Rig and me'll pay you back."

"Sure will," Rig Bogan echoed. "Say, let's go have another look at that beautiful new wagon of ours." He downed the drink in his hand and led the way eagerly out of the saloon.

"I'll be getting back to my desk," the banker told Buchanan. "Good luck in your new venture."

"Thanks."

"And keep a tight rein on that partner of yours," Penney added in a worried undertone. "I tell you frankly, if I had known Bogan's background when we started negotiations, I doubt whether I would have taken the risk."

"Rig's straightened out," Buchanan said. "He's out of prison to stay."

"Let's hope so," the little banker said fervently. "But keep a close haul on him. And watch his drinking."

"Sure," Buchanan promised and turned to follow Bogan up the street. A smile touched the big man's lips as he recalled Penney's words. What the moneyman also hadn't known a month ago was that he was their last chance, that every other lender in San Antone had turned them down flat.

Not that it made one whit of difference to Tom Buchanan whether he got into the freighting business or didn't. The whole venture, as a matter of fact, was in the nature of a favor for Rig's old daddy, the sheriff of Alpine in West Texas. Buchanan had run into Jessie Bogan during one of his infrequent visits to the Big Bend country a year back.

"How's your boy Rig?" he'd asked sociably and the lawman's expression had clouded over.

"Rig's serving time in Huntsville Prison," Jessie had told him bleakly. "Killed a man in a knife fight over to Hondo. Killed him over a woman."

"What I know of Hondo," Buchanan had said, "that ain't so special. Thirty days in the pokey, maybe, but not shipped off to Huntsville."

"This was special," Bogan Senior had said. "The woman was this man's wife. And he caught Rig dead to rights in his own bedroom."

"Well, yeah," Buchanan had had to agree,

10

embarrassed for the old man.

"And the knife didn't help none," the sheriff had added with some bitterness. "Never knew a Texas jury to let up on a knifer."

"Guess not," Buchanan had agreed again. "When does Rig get out?"

"Six months. But I had to find that out on my own, same as the rest of the story. The boy hasn't written me a line."

"Figured to spare you."

"You reckon?"

"Sure."

The next day Jessie Bogan had invited Buchanan to take supper with him at the Alpine House. The sheriff had been in a remembering mood and he spoke of the men, good and bad, who had made his career such a colorful one in the Big Bend. Then, out of the blue: "You still got the wanderlust, big fella, or are you fixin' to settle down?"

"I'm moving on," Buchanan had admitted, smiling, knowing that all sheriffs, everywhere, disapproved on principle of the restless breed.

"Which direction this time?" Jessie Bogan had asked.

Buchanan had shrugged his great shoulders. "Seen California from tip to top," he said. "Thought I might have a look at New Orleans. Met a fella in Paso last winter, gamblin' man. Told me he had a proposition if I was ever in his town."

"What kind of proposition?" the sheriff had asked hawkishly.

"Same old thing," Buchanan had said. "His money, my gun."

"Got yourself honed pretty slick, have ya?" Bogan had snapped, making Buchanan grin again.

"Not so slick as you, Mr. Jess," he'd said.

"Bosh! Half the rannies I had to plug outdrew me. It's lookin' at the badge that unsteadies 'em. Hope you never shoot a peace officer, Tom Buchanan!"

"Hope I never have to, Sheriff."

Bogan had studied that broad, broken-nosed face across the table and some of the sharpness went out of his own. "So you're bound for the fleshpots of New Orleans?" he'd asked, switching the subject back abruptly.

"Going in that general direction. If I get there it'll be in easy stages."

"Got San Antone on your itinerary?"

"Not especially, Mr. Jess. Why?"

"Got a notion about my boy," the sheriff had said. "A hunch he might head there himself when he gets out of Huntsville."

"Pretty close to Hondo don't you think?"

Bogan had nodded. "Too damn close. But I been writin' back and forth to Warden Almy, an old friend of mine. He told me that Rig gets mail regular from a woman name of Ruth Stell. From an address in San Antone." The man's face had darkened. "Sam Stell," he said, "happens to be the man Rig knifed to death."

Buchanan had nodded. He'd seen no reason to comment.

"So I figure that's where Rig will go first thing," Bogan had gone on. "And I was also thinkin' that if you happened to be in that neck of the woods six months from now you might look the boy up."

"Sure will, if I am," Buchanan had told him.

"Couldn't make it any more definite than that, though?"

The big man had looked puzzled. "Mr. Jess," he'd said then, "if you've got something you want me to tell Rig for you, why I'll make it a point to be in San Antone."

Then, for the first time, Bogan had smiled. He'd seemed very relieved by Buchanan's offer.

"I'm askin' for somethin' more than that, Tom. I'm askin' you to stick with him for a spell, see him settled down into some honest work."

"Me?" Buchanan had laughed. "A fine example I'd make."

"Rig'd listen to anything you told him to do. That boy thinks the sun rises and sets on your account alone." As the old man spoke he had reached inside his vest and then he'd withdrawn a worn, mildewed leather billfold. He'd laid the thing in front of Buchanan. "Half of what's inside is for you, Tom," he'd said. "Half is for my son."

Buchanan had looked into the wallet. He'd counted ten gold certificates, each worth a hundred dollars. He removed half of them, folded them over and stuck them in the pocket of his shirt. Then slid the wallet back across the table.

"No charge for friendship," he'd told the other man but Bogan had shaken his head vigorously, pushed the money toward him again.

"It's yours, son, to do with as you see fit. I won't have it any other way."

Nor would he. So, when Buchanan arrived in San Antone — after a six-month stint herding beef along the Rio Grande — he had the thousand intact in his kick plus an extra two hundred. In the first two saloons he was given the same information: they knew Rig Bogan, all right, but until he settled his bar bill and stopped his everlasting brawling he was not welcome in either place.

". . . and stranger, if that worthless tramp owes you money, too, then you'll just have to take it out of his hide."

In both places Buchanan settled the accounts, a total of sixty dollars, and when he inquired in the third saloon the name that Jessie Bogan had mentioned came back to him.

"Do you know a lady name of Ruth Stell?" he asked and the bartender snickered unpleasantly.

"A lady, no," he answered. "But there's a Ruthie works down to Queenie's place."

"Works at what?"

"Oldest work there is, mister."

"And where is Queenie's?"

"Down in La Villita, the Spanish section." He smiled crookedly. "You won't have to look for it," he said, "you'll hear it coming."

Buchanan did hear it, four blocks away — blaring music, sporadic gunfire, squealing girls and shouting men. A great, gaudy pile of wood was Queenie's, four stories high, where four different businesses were being run at the same time, under the same roof, and each one going full blast. Every seat at every gambling table was taken, every foot of dance floor was in use, they clamored three deep at the sixty-foot bar and the procession going up and down the wide staircase to the rooms above was about as continuous as Buchanan had seen since he'd left San Francisco.

And surveying it all from a balcony high on one wall, gazing down like some pagan goddess, was absolutely the grossest, ugliest accumulation of female flesh ever stuffed into a tentlike, black beaded gown.

15

Absolutely, Buchanan told himself judiciously, looking at her with the same frank wonder that his own appearance nearly always occasioned.

His concentration was broken by a hand pulling insistently on his arm and he glanced down into a pair of mischievous brown eyes, an apple-cheeked face and a ripe young figure enclosed in a green silk dress that eliminated all speculation.

"Hey, big honey," she shouted above the din, "how about me?"

"You Ruth Stell?"

"I'm Lotti-Mae, big honey! And all yours . . ."

"Show me Ruth Stell, would you?"

"Find her yourself," Lottie-Mae said sulkily and flounced off with her tailgate carried high. Buchanan shouldered his way to a place at the jampacked bar, ordered a beer from the sweating, bad-tempered barman. His nickel was scooped up.

"Wait a minute, friend."

"Now what?"

"Which one is Ruth Stell?"

"Jesus Christ! Fifty chippies floating around and I'm supposed to . . ."

"Hey, where's that drink I ordered?" a voice bellowed and the bartender fled. Buchanan tried a waiter next, a young Mex, but the boy only shrugged his thin shoulders and hurried his full tray to the gam-

16

bling section. Then Buchanan was being asked for information by a slim, silky-voiced man in a tailored black jacket and string bowtie.

"What's our problem tonight, cowboy?" he asked and Buchanan got the definite impression that brush poppers were this fellow's social inferiors.

"Why, no problem, dudey," he said softly. "Unless you brought one with you."

"Queenie's been watching you," the man told him, the slightest edge in his tone. "Queenie says for a nickel beer you're disrupting a lot of service and on top of that she don't like the way you stared at her when you came in."

Buchanan swung his back on the man and raised his glance to the woman on the balcony again. "What does the queen bee weigh, you reckon?" he asked aloud.

"Cowboy," came the tight reply, "you're looking up at the best lip reader in all the States and Territories — see what I mean?"

"I saw her move her ten chins up and down. What does that mean?"

"It means you're leaving the premises immediate."

Buchanan looked back over his shoulder at the man, grinned wickedly.

"What'll you bet?" he asked him.

"Lay you six to one," was the confident answer. "And I ain't lost yet." His dark,

17

cynical eyes were watching something developing beyond Buchanan and the big man turned to see it, too.

One, two, three, four, five he counted. Five scowling, dull-eyed beef-eaters bearing down on him in a group, in cadence, one simple idea in their collective mind. The dancers stopped dancing, opened up to let them through. The music faded away. The mob at the bar swung silently to watch and even the sound of clinking chips and whirring roulette wheels ceased, for the regulars knew that rarely, rarely did Queenie send her whole riot squad against a single offender.

"You said six to one," Buchanan was saying conversationally to the man at his back. "You including yourself in on the doin's?"

"If it comes to that, cowboy. Now why don't you just about face and walk out of here with your health?"

"I like the bet," Buchanan said cheerfully. "A hundred dollars worth?"

"You're faded." The five of them were there then, forming a truculent, slavish semi-circle around the object of Queenie's disfavor. Buchanan looked into each face, his grin grown broader, wilder. Behind him the dapper houseman was exchanging a last glance with the balcony, spread his arms expressively. Queenie's chins jiggled up and down

18

with great eagerness.

"Put him in the street, boys," said the silken voice. "Hard!"

The first surprise was a tactical one. By ancient tradition the bouncer attacks the troublemaker. The troublemaker's role is a defensive one, delaying tactics, commit as much damage in retreat as he is able. He is, also, by tradition, either very drunk or very angry. Buchanan was neither. He was joyously sober, in a gala mood, and the prospect of a good rough and tumble after six hard, dull months herding cattle brought a thunderous, rather frightening roar of laughter bursting from the depths of his chest.

On that note he waded in, having chosen Numher three, in the middle, as his first objective. He caught him in the middle, too, marking the soft bellies on all of them, and with his left fist buried wrist-deep into flesh he clubbed the man senseless with a short, choppy, overhand right. Number four never got his hands up, either. He stepped flat-footed, in fact, into a hard, straight left that had all of Buchanan's incredible shoulder driving it.

Now speed was everything, and he was a blur of motion as he swung on Numbers one and two, wrapped his great hands around their thick necks and brought their skulls crashing together with a sickening sound that carried loud and clear to the gawking, open-mouthed spectator in the balcony seat.

Buchanan let them drop, turned leisurely, expectantly to Number five. But that one had seen enough and he wasn't having any. Not for any forty a month. He backed off, hands upraised before him as though Buchanan carried two guns rather than fists, almost tripped clumsily over one of his unconscious friends, then whirled and broke into full retreat.

From the bar came a loud, warm-sounding cheer and Buchanan waved a greeting. "Drink 'er down, boys," he invited. "I got six hundred dollars coming!" But as he turned to collect the bet the smile faded from his face and the blue eyes grew dangerously chill. The slim houseman had drawn a two-barrelled Derringer, had it leveled at Buchanan's heart

"You ain't won a thing, cowboy," he said tensely. "Get out or get killed —"

A six-gun roared three times, and three times the man's body jerked convulsively. He was dead as he fell to the floor. A dark-bearded, heavy-set individual stepped from his place at the bar, holstering the Colt as he came.

"Obliged to you," Buchanan said.

"Hell, fun is fun," that one growled, rolling the dead man on his back with the toe of his boot. "What'd you say the snake owed you?"

"That debt's paid, friend."

"Anything else you need?"

"Yeh," Buchanan said, "an introduction to Ruth Stell."

His new friend looked around at the silently staring crowd, pointed his arm at a brunette woman who had been dancing. "Step over here, Ruthie," he commanded, "and meet a man for a change."

Ruth Stell hesitated, looked to the balcony for instructions. But Queenie, white-faced, kept her own gaze riveted on Buchanan.

"Come on, Ruthie," the bearded man shouted. "Since when are you so bashful?" The brunette moved from her companion, came toward them with an expression of defiance and a confident sway of hips that was obviously feigned.

"You lookin' for me?" she asked tartly. Buchanan found a kind of prettiness in her face, but hardness, too, and a whore's calculating eyes. Her best attraction was her figure, but the tall man doubted if it was worth a hitch in Huntsville.

"You seen enough?" she snapped, a hand on her hip.

Buchanan nodded. "Where can I find Rig Bogan?" he asked.

Suspicion flooded her. "What's Rig to you?"

"A kid I used to know."

"Well, he aint no kid now."

"So I hear. Where can I find him?"

"He don't want to see anybody."

"He'll want to see me," Buchanan said. "I got something for him."

"What?"

"Money," he said, and smiled at the magic change that worked.

"Well, why didn't you say so?" she said in an entirely new voice. "Come on, I'll take you to him."

She had attached herself to his arm like an eager leech, but Buchanan held back for another moment, extended his hand to the bearded man.

"The name's Buchanan," he told him, "and I hope I can return the favor."

"I'm Jeb Wilson," the man said in his gruff way, "and you can do yourself a favor by staying away from that Bogan maverick. Nothin' but a drunk and a deadbeat."

Of all the estimates of Jess Bogan's boy that Buchanan had heard, this one from Jeb Wilson counted the hardest. Rig was more even than a fellow West Texan. He was Big Bend, born and raised, and Buchanan's best recollection of him was a friendly, gangling, freckled-kid that his own bunch, two and three years older, let tag along on whatever business they were about. He was the sheriff's son and that gave him a certain stand-

22

ing, but to hear what he had made of himself was a real discouragement.

"There's going to be a change in Rig Bogan," Buchanan told Jeb Wilson. "You'll be proud to know him, one day soon."

"Could be," Wilson said, gazing around the floor at the wreckage of Queenie's feared riot squad. "I saw something else happen tonight that I didn't believe possible."

Buchanan bid him good-by, tipped his Stetson toward the balcony in a good-natured gesture of peace, and let Ruthie Stell lead him out. When they reached the street he quite expected they would turn uptown, but they went left, instead, deeper into the dark and unpromising heart of La Villita. They came, finally, to a shabby gray frame house — a sagging shack, really — and she started inside.

"He lives here?" Buchanan asked, wondering how any Alpine son could choose this when he had the whole Texas sky for a roof.

"I live here," the girl said. "Rig sort of boards, but I never see no rent money." She pushed the creaking door open and Buchanan followed her into the musty-smelling room. He rnade out the outline of a table in the darkness, two chairs.

"Rig?" she called aloud into the opening of the other room. "Company come to call, Rig!" There was no answer from beyond. "I'll go wake him if I can," she said. "What'd you say your name was?"

"Tell him it's Tom Buchanan. From old Alpine."

She went in there and he could hear her talking to him, urgently, saying "Tom Buchanan" and "Alpine" and "Got money for you, baby." And a voice he had to assume was Rig Bogan's was murmuring groggily, unintelligibly. She kept at him with persistence, and after another full minute a man's form appeared in the doorway. Not so tall as Buchanan, but taller than most men, and Buchanan tried to associate it with the tagalong kid of other, more carefree days.

"Hello, Rig," Buchanan said, his voice sounding especially deep and resonant in this small dark place.

"What the hell do you want with me?" Bogan answered, the drink and sleep making his own voice furry.

"Come on and take a walk outside," Buchanan said, deciding that now was not the time to tell the other man his mission in San Antone.

"Ruthie said you had money for me . . ."

"Let's walk a while."

"Walk, hell! I walked for two straight years in Huntsville. Or ain't you heard about that?"

"I heard, Rig."

"Yeah? Who told you?"

"Your daddy told me."

"Pa?" he said, stricken-sounding. "Oh, Jesus, how'd Pa hear it?"

"Lawmen write back and forth. That's what you should have done . . ."

"Let's get to the money," Ruthie said, lighting one candle and then a second. Buchanan stared unhappily at what he saw of Rig Bogan now and what he remembered of some ten years ago. Unshaven, haggard-eyed, gone slack around the mouth. He even had to lean against the door frame for support. And the clothes on his back looked as though they hadn't been washed or aired for a month.

"Rig," Buchanan said with his natural candor, "you look like hell."

"Who asked you anyhow?"

"Just give him his money," Ruthie said, "and leave him be. I know how to take care of him."

Buchanan's glance was sardonic. "Don't do me the same favor, ma'am," he requested.

"Give Rig his money," she repeated.

"There is no money," Buchanan told her.

"You said there was!"

"Figured that would make you cooperate some. Come on, Rig, let's get some fresh air."

"Oh no you don't!" the girl said angrily.

"You give him his money right here where I can see it . . ."

"You didn't marry this boy, did you?"

"No, I'm not married to him. But I been keeping him ever since he got out of prison and I'm entitled to my share!"

"You do any share of his two years at Huntsville?"

"What?"

"Story I heard," the big man said quietly, "Rig did his time on your account. Maybe you owe him a lot of keeping."

"I don't owe him a goddamn thing! Was it my fault that stingy old man got back from Abilene a night earlier? Did I put the knife in Rig's hand and tell him to use it?"

"I wasn't there, ma'am," Buchanan said. "Come on, Rig . . ."

"Wait a minute, wait a minute," Bogan said, straightening his body and taking a step toward Ruthie. "What the hell do you mean, you didn't put the knife in my hand?"

"I didn't!"

Bogan's liquored eyes widened. "By Christ, you believe it, don't you? You believe the story we made up . . ."

"Nothing was made up! You had me on the bed and Sam came in! He said some mean, nasty things and you killed him!"

"He said for you to take the dress you got married in and get out of his house," Rig

26

told her in a monotone. "I was drunk but I remember that. Next thing I knew I had a knife, and you were screaming your head off and pushing me toward the old man . . ."

"Lies, lies!" she screamed now and Buchanan had his own opinion of how it could have been that wild night. "You're a dirty, lying sonofabitch!"

An animal sound broke from Bogan's throat, but before he could get at her Buchanan's arm encircled his chest, held him off.

"How about that fresh air, old buddy?" he asked him.

"Yeah," Rig said. "It suddenly sounds real good."

"Go on, get out!" Ruthie screeched furiously. "And don't think you're ever coming back! Not if you crawl to me on your knees!"

"Don't hold your breath till that happens, ma'am," Buchanan advised her. "This boy don't know the meaning of the word." He took Bogan out of there, with her voice following them clear up the street, and then it was gratefully silent, with a comfortable silence between the two men. Finally Rig broke it.

"Crazy," he said.

"What is?"

"Ruthie. Ruthie believing that story about

the knife. Hell, she made it up her own self that very night."

"Forget it, Rig. You're square with the law and you're square with her. Startin' a clean slate."

Bogan laughed, sounding for a moment like the one he knew in the Big Bend. "The warden said something like that the day I left," he said. "It sounds different coming from you."

TWO

BUCHANAN HAD TAKEN a room at the San Antonio Hotel, but for a reason he didn't bother to explain to himself that night he bought an extra blanket, rented a horse for Rig, loaded supplies on a pack mule and took off for the Plateau. Bogan didn't protest the trip, asked no questions, and though he slept fitfully beneath the stars, he was up at dawn when the aroma of fresh eggs, bacon, and strong coffee revived old memories of camping out.

They spent the morning fishing trout out of the cold mountain stream, hunted in the afternoon. Rig had the Winchester at the start, but when he missed his first four chances he trade the rifle for Buchanan's Colt. He couldn't hit with Old Reliable, either.

"What I wouldn't give for a drink," he said shakily.

"Here," Buchanan said, offering his canteen.

"Who the hell wants water, man?"

"Not me," Buchanan grinned. "That's why I filled this with straight Kentucky bourbon." Bogan took the canteen, sniffed it suspiciously, then drank.

"Had you figured wrong, Buchanan," he said then. "Figured you took me up here for the holy roll."

"Pass the jug, boy, to a thirsty man," Buchanan told him, taking the canteen and tilting it in direct proportion to his size.

"You drink regular?" Bogan asked.

"Every chance I get."

"Don't seem to bother you none. Not — not like some fellas."

"Well, I learned me a good trick about whisky."

"A trick?"

"Don't ever drink whisky when things are going bad," Buchanan said sagely. "A beer, maybe, just to cut the dust. But the red eye only when the going is good."

"Yeah," Bogan said thoughtfully, "but how do you keep things going good?" and Buchanan laughed uproariously.

"That," he said with glee, "is another trick altogether."

That brought Bogan into the little joke, and Buchanan noted with satisfaction that his laughter was genuine, unrestrained. It sounded like it might have been a long time since the other man had had a reason to laugh. They passed the canteen back and forth until it was dry, rode back to their campsite, ate a huge supper and were asleep in their blankets before eight o'clock.

They lived in the mountains for the next forty-five days, took their survival from the land when Buchanan's supplies gave out, and the change in Rig Bogan was marvelous. At least Buchanan thought so, though not a direct word on the subject passed his lips.

On the morning, for instance, that his "patient" decided on his own hook to shave, Buchanan commented that seeing the freckles again was the first time he was sure that this was the bona fide Rig Bogan and not an imposter. That was the same morning Rig washed his clothes, went about the camp stark naked until they dried and earned himself the nickname "Apollo" for the next week.

And when Bogan's nerves steadied down, when he could sight and fire the rifle and the revolver with some semblance of his Big Bend learning, ride out alone and return with his share of the next day's food — even then Buchanan's praise was on the light side and wryly humorous, never indicative of the deep pride he felt in the other man's rehabilitation.

He considered his own role in the affair as of relatively small importance, as a happy chain of events that reunited two boyhood chums again, for Buchanan sincerely believed that, sooner or later, Rig

Bogan would have halted his downhill slide on his own and made the same physical and mental recovery that he'd achieved during these past six weeks.

But even though he declined any credit, Buchanan still thought it wiser not to tell Rig he was worth a thousand dollars. He thought so because he was afraid Rig would misjudge his present poverty against the thousand and think he had a lot of rnoney. Which he didn't. It was only good for what Mr. Jess had said, to get him settled down into some honest work.

So Buchanan kept mum and waited hopefully. And on the forty-fourth day his hopes were answered.

"Jezuz," Rig said during dinner. "Jezuz, I wish I had me a little money."

"What would you do with money?" Buchanan joshed.

"I'd buy me a wagon, that's what. And mules."

"You? Driving a wagon?"

"It's a damn good business," Bogan said with some warmth. "Especially out of San Antone, with all that Mexican trade."

"Yeh?" Buchanan asked doubtfully.

"I know what I'm talking about," Bogan insisted. "That's what I was doing when I met Ruthie, driving a wagon. Full load down and a full load back."

"Your own wagon?"

Bogan shook his head. "The Argus Express Company," he said. "But I was starting to save up for my own. Not a big one or anything fancy. Just a little old wagon, painted bright red." His face saddened. "Then I met Ruthie on the Hondo run. Seems like everything went bad from then on."

"How much does a wagon cost?"

"Oh, five or six hundred. Another hundred for mules."

"How much would you make on a trip?"

"Well, you wouldn't want to take a little wagon clear down into Mexico," Bogan explained. "You'd run a kind of shuttle service."

"How much would you make?" Buchanan asked again.

"A living," Bogan answered. "In a year or two you'd be doing real good."

"A year or two?" Buchanan echoed gloomily. "What about a three-team wagon?"

"Six mules? Why, man, that's where the big money is. You take a load of cotton, and hoes, and axes — everything they're yammering for down there — and you clean up. Course," he added, "you got to slip past the damn customs."

"How come?"

"How come? Because those thieving Mex politicians and generals want their cut. Just about wipes out your profit before you make final delivery of the shipment."

"A little smuggling on the side, that it?"

Bogan shrugged. "Everybody does it," he said. "Sometimes you get caught and sometimes you don't."

"And if you do?"

"Well, first they fine you. Take your wagon and your goods. Then they shoot you."

Buchanan, who probably knew as much about smuggling as any man on either side of the Rio Grande, was not asking his questions to seek information. He was listening to Bogan's tone of enthusiasm, studying the younger fellow's sincerity.

"Sounds chancey to me, Rig," he told him now.

"Sure, and that's why the payoff's so big. But what the hell difference does it make? I can't even make the down payment on a wheel, let alone a team of mules."

"Forget those one-team wagons," Buchanan said. "Takes too long. How much is six mules and a wagon?"

"Why?"

"Because you and me got a thousand to invest."

"You and me — a *thousand?*"

"If you want to go into the freight business, and I guess it's as good as any."

"You mean we'll buy a wagon?"

"Start at the top," Buchanan grinned, "and work our way down."

He told Rig Bogan the story of the money then, of the meeting with old Jessie back in Alpine, and in the morning they rode down out of the Plateau and started their almost futile search for a loan that would put them in business.

And this morning they had their wagon, a thing of beauty to Rig and painted about the reddest red Buchanan had ever seen. DOUBLE-B FAST FREIGHT, it said on either side in bold white letters. T. BUCHANAN — R. BOGAN — OWNERS. WAGON No. 1.

"Ain't she the prettiest thing ever?" Rig wanted to know, running his hand over the smooth panel. "Sure gonna break my heart the first mud we slosh through."

"Mr. Penney won't mind, though," Buchanan said.

"Look yonder, Tom," Bogan said, his voice urgent. "I think I see our first customer."

Buchanan turned to find a portly, prosperous-looking gent making his way into the yard. "You know him, Rig?"

"Honest John Magee," Bogan told him. "Biggest cotton broker in the market. Better let me do the negotiatin', partner."

"Help yourself, only don't drive too hard a bargain the first time."

Honest John Magee came up to them and surveyed each man silently from head to toe.

"My name is Magee," he said then, curtly,

speaking directly to Buchanan. "When can you leave for Matamoros?"

"Mr. Bogan handles those details," Buchanan said.

"I know all about Mr. Bogan," the broker said. "I'm asking you. When can you take my cotton to Matamoros?"

"Well, about five minutes, I guess. That right, Rig?"

"There's a few other matters to discuss first," Rig said importantly. "Do you want this cotton shipped on a commission basis?"

"I pay a dollar a mile," Magee told Buchanan. "Take it or leave it."

Buchanan looked at Bogan. Rig said, "Do we take this through customs at Matamoros or slip across the river at Olmito?"

"Honest John Magee isn't in the smuggling trade. He pays the legal tariff."

"In that case, Mr. Magee," Rig said, "we'd prefer to take this on a ten per cent commission."

"A dollar a mile," Magee snapped at Buchanan. "Take it or leave it!"

"Payable when?"

"Half now, half when I see the invoices signed by Manuel Gomez of Matamoros."

"Rig?"

Bogan shrugged.

"You got a deal, Magee," Buchanan told him. "Where do we pick up the goods?"

"At my warehouse. Good day to you." The rich broker strode away, full of his own importance, and the two partners watched his exit with a kind of embarrassed silence between them.

Buchanan spoke into it.

"Makes a lot of noise, don't he?"

"Yeh."

"Didn't rile you, did he?"

"Some," Bogan admitted, his voice subdued. "Guess I got a lot more atoning to do in this town."

"To hell with that, boy," Buchanan told him. "You can strut the yard like any rooster present."

"No I can't. If it'd been Bogan's Fast Freight old Magee wouldn't've trusted me to deliver an old sow to Austin."

"Tell you what we'll do, pard," Buchanan said. "We'll let old Honest John deliver his own damn cotton to Matamoros. We don't need him."

"Yes we do, Tom. That's a three-hundred-dollar job. And if he don't fill the wagon I can maybe wangle a couple or three small shipments extra. Another fifty dollars, maybe, not to mention a full load coming back up from Brownsville and Corpus Christi. We need Magee real bad."

Buchanan grinned, slapped him on the back. Talk like that was music to the big man's ears, reassured him of Bogan's new

37

hold on life, meant that the time was coming soon when he himself could fade out of the picture, leave this dull freighting business and resume his natural life again.

"Well," he said happily, "let's go pick up the damn cotton then. And whatever else these mules are gonna haul to Mexico."

"One thing first, though, Tom."

"What's that?"

"I'd admire to handle our first job myself."

"Why don't we both take the trip?"

"That ain't good business," Bogan said. "When one partner's on the road the other one's busy at headquarters lining up more jobs."

"Well, if that's the way it's done. But I'd be glad to flip you for the chore."

"I don't look on it like a chore, Tom. I know you don't really have much heart for freighting . . ."

"Sure I do!"

"You ain't foolin' me none," Rig said. "Business matters don't suit you. Sittin' on a highboard behind six slow mules ain't your style."

"Boy, you don't know some of the work I've done. Not by half . . ."

"But I like freighting," Bogan went on. "Sounds strange from Jessie Bogan's son, but I'd rather pull freight from one place to another than anything else I can think of."

"That's fine, Rig. That's great!"

"Then there's no objection to my driving this shipment?"

"Not from this hoss," Buchanan said and a smile of relief came over his face. "Truth be known, Rig, I was dreadin' the prospect."

They drove together to load Magee's cotton, and Buchanan rode along while Rig made a tour of the depots, talking fast and picking up consignments of odds and ends that crammed every last square inch of the red wagon. They returned to the little office of the Double-B Fast Freight Company then and had a drink for a smooth journey.

"Don't see how you can miss, Rig," Buchanan told him warmly. "You've got the stuff."

"Thanks to a couple of gents," Bogan said. "You and my Pa."

"Ever write to him?"

"Going to," he said. "Enclosing a draft on Mr. Penney's bank for one thousand dollars, signed by R. Bogan. Never wrote one. Have you?"

"Hell, no, I haven't," Buchanan laughed. "Nor cashed one. I ain't even used to these gold certificates."

"Can't beat hard money," Bogan agreed, setting down his glass on a filing cabinet. "Well, partner," he said then, "I got to go see Señor Manuel Gomez, Matamoros, Mexico." He extended his hand and Buchanan's enveloped it.

"Sure you don't want company?"

"Positive. You just line up a payload for the Double-B and have it ready to go in about eight days from now."

"That's when you'll be back?"

"Approximate," Bogan said. "With the wagon jam-packed."

Buchanan saw him off, watched until the red wagon was just a speck in the distance, then walked back into the office, feeling strange and restless, looking all about himself and wondering what the hell he was supposed to do now. He looked at the shiny new desk with a perplexed expression, approached it warily and then, just to see what it felt like, carefully lowered his six-and-a-half-foot frame into the chair.

How? he marveled. How do they do it? He could hear old Penney — "I'll be getting back to my desk" — and sitting behind this one he wondered how a man could do it. Yet they were everywhere, in every town he'd ever visited. Hundreds and hundreds of them, thousands and thousands — living, breathing men who spent their entire lives trapped in a chair like this one, staring at four white walls and a ceiling, not knowing what it was to be your own man in this big, wonderful country. And free.

Buchanan got himself out of that chair, quick, and was on his way clear out of the office when the door burst open and

40

flushed, angry-eyed Honest John Magee confronted him.

"So, by God, it is true!" the man roared.

Buchanan frowned, cocked his head quizzically.

"I thought I made it clear," Magee raged, "that my cotton was consigned to you!" He pointed a finger accusingly at Buchanan's eyes. "You!" he repeated. "Not that shiftless, double-dealing ex-convict you've taken up with." The loud voice trailed away and some protective sixth sense warned it to hold still. The threatening finger, an effective weapon everywhere else in San Antonio, was meekly withdrawn. For there had once been a night, around a poker table in Dodge, and Honest John had seen a man look at another the way this tall man was looking down at him. Something about the way the cards were dealt, Magee recalled very vividly now, and violence had followed swiftly.

"Bogan," Magee said in a subdued, conciliatory tone, "has a poor reputation in this town."

"Bogan's my partner," Buchanan answered. "His rep is mine."

"I'd still feel better if you were delivering my cotton."

"Mister," Buchanan told him, "Bogan will be back here in eight days. And you've got the privilege of buying the first drink."

41

"Is that what he said, eight days?"

"Right."

"I wish I had your confidence in him," Magee said.

"Just have the cork out of the bottle," Buchanan replied and the worried broker turned and walked out.

That next week was a drag. Buchanan came to the freight yard each morning at seven, entered the office and sat there for as long as he could stand it. Then he would prowl the streets of San Antone, restlessly, without purpose, and the sight of the huge, shoulder-swinging figure made many an onlooker think uneasily of a brooding lion being loose among them.

Buchanan was also of some concern to the local law, Marshal Grieve. Like most good peace officers in a melting pot of a town like this one, Fred Grieve was a reformed drifter and border rider himself. He could spot the type at a glance, that wildness, the easy bravado, and he had alerted his twelve constables for something special in the way of trouble half an hour after the big man rode in and began asking for Rig Bogan. Buchanan had made a true prophet of the lawman by his performance in Queenie's over in Spanishtown. That was as special as you could ask for, even in San Antone, and Grieve had called in his off-duty force, waited for the twister to really rip.

But then the perplexing things had happened, the contradictions that disturbed the marshal deeply. Instead of leading the fractious Bogan into real trouble, the drifter had taken the ex-convict out of town altogether, up into the Plateau, his two trailers reported. Waiting for the rest to gather, Grieve decided, and waited himself for a raid on one of the banks. But no. Six weeks go by and the two friends return — Bogan so tanned and fit he was almost unrecognizable — and though they visited the banks, and other merchants, there was nothing against the law in trying to borrow money.

Then surprise number two. The Double-B Fast Freight, red wagon, yard, office and all. If Fred Grieve was a betting man, and if he had a hundred dollars, you would have gotten long odds that no breed of tomcat like this Buchanan from West Texas would ever get mired down in the freight business. But, by the harry, he was — and with no less than Honest John Magee for a customer.

Last of the contradictions about Buchanan, and probably the most unsettling to a plain-thinking, plain-speaking man like the marshal, was that he had yet to see the other man packing the tool of his trade. Grieve admitted, only to himself, that he could have made a few minor errors in judgment about Buchanan's purposes in coming to San Antone. But not about Buchanan being a gunfighter. He couldn't be wrong about that.

So the marshal asked him, stopped him in the middle of State Street and put it to him pointblank. This was the afternoon of the fourth day that Rig Bogan had driven out with the wagon.

"What's your game, bucko?" Grieve asked, and Buchanan looked from the silver badge to the leathery face in surprise. A moment before being accosted his mind had been full of thoughts about New Orleans, the prospect of busy days and busier nights, a life where a man had something to occupy himself. Not, by God, this owning a damn freight business.

"My *game?*" he said to the marshal.

"You own a gun, don't you?"

"Yeh."

"And you know how to use it, don't you?"

Buchanan nodded.

"And if someone needed that gun real bad," Grieve went on, "they could hire it, couldn't they?"

"You mean to say with all those constables of yours . . ."

"Hell, I ain't talking about *me* hiring it."

"Then what are you talking about?"

"About you," the marshal said. "You might have sold Magee and Penney on you being a freighter, bucko, but you don't fool me for two minutes."

"What do you figure I'm up to, marshal?"

"It'll develop soon, I expect. Your kind don't play the waiting game for long. But when it happens," Grieve told him, "I'll be right there to take a hand. Remember it."

Buchanan smiled. "Fair enough," he said. "Thanks for the advance notice."

"Welcome. And you can start packing that shooter anytime. Get your cards out where folks can see them." Grieve left Buchanan standing in the middle of State Street, walked away with the feeling that he had scored some victory over the big man. Buchanan shrugged off the conversation and continued his restless tour.

The fifth day passed. The sixth. The seventh. Buchanan was at the yard and waiting as dawn appeared on the morning of the eighth day. In his mind he went over the little speech he had prepared for Rig, the one in which he turned over the business and wished him luck. Rig would protest some, try to give him some money, but to no avail. Then Rig would understand that the best thing he could do for him was to let him be on his way.

Mid-morning came, passed into afternoon, and there was no sign of Rig. The

45

northbound stage pulled in but the driver had seen nothing of a red freight wagon.

"Remember passing it a week or so ago," the fellow said. "Going south with a load of cotton. That the one?"

That was the one all right. Shadows grew longer, dusk fell, and a disappointed Buchanan bought himself a quart of bourbon and took it to the bar at the San Antonio Hotel. The bottle was some two fingers lighter when company arrived.

"I see you're buying the first drink," Honest John Magee said pointedly.

"Help yourself, mister," Buchanan told him glumly. "He'll be here tomorrow, sure."

"Will he?"

"Bright and early. He knows he's expected."

Magee downed his drink, raised his eyes to Buchanan's face. "Bogan ever tell you about working for the Argus Express Company?" the broker asked in a careful voice.

"Sure he did. Why?"

"Ever say why he was fired?"

"On account of the trouble he got into — killing that fellow in Hondo . . . ."

Magee was shaking his head. "He was fired a month before that happened," he said. "For stealing."

Buchanan studied the speaker. "I hope you can back that up," he said quietly.

"The law was never brought into it,"

Magee answered. "It was settled quietly by Amos Ferguson, who owned Argus, and Bogan. Seemed that Amos knew Bogan's father from someplace. A sheriff, isn't he?"

Buchanan nodded. "What was Rig accused of stealing?"

"A shipment of axes. A wagonload of them. His story was that he was jumped by agents between here and Hondo. A story that didn't hold up so far as old Amos was concerned."

"Why not?"

Magee poured them both a drink. "A fellow comes to you with patches in his britches and you give him a job for seven dollars a week. His room and board are five, and he buys himself some boots and work clothes. Then a load he's delivering gets hijacked. Axes. Easy to get rid of and impossible to identify."

"So?"

"So you happen to be over in Hondo one Saturday night. Sitting at a dark table in the back of this saloon is this seven-a-week driver of yours. He's sitting with this married woman and they're drinking good whisky, not beer. And instead of those work pants and worn boots he's sporting an outfit that must have cost sixty dollars. And when he leaves the place he and the woman drive off in a brand new shiny rig. Well, what would you think happened to those axes?"

Buchanan seemed absorbed in the three interlocking circles his finger was tracing on the bartop. But Magee hadn't invented any story about Rig. Why should he? And the little he had seen of Ruthie Stell was enough to know that she was the woman men like Bogan turn bad over. Buchanan met the other man's gaze, looked deep into it.

"You figure your cotton is gone?" he asked him.

"It was worth ten thousand in gold to my customer in Matamoros," Magee replied. "That's an awful lot of temptation for the wrong man."

Buchanan set his empty glass down, swung away.

"Where you going?" Magee called after him.

"South, mister. To Matamoros. But I *will* be back."

"I know you will," the broker said.

Buchanan rode out of San Antone within twenty minutes. On his hip rode a Colt. In the saddle boot was a Winchester. Marshal Grieve watched him go with satisfaction.

"That," he said aloud, "is more natural."

48

THREE

IN A COUNTRY of big men, they called this one Big Red. In a fierce society where only the strongest had the right to lead, no man of his band ever challenged the rule of Big Red Leech. And it had been that way for three years now, ever since the end of the war when Leech, with customary boldness, declared that his personal spoils of victory was the deserted mission near El Indio. Rechristened Fort Leech, fortified with cannon and manned by ten hand-picked veterans of the First Missouri Cavalry, Leech sallied forth from this stronghold to pillage, rob, rape and kidnap the Mexican population for fifty miles around. Those who could move out of the region did so in terror. Those who couldn't, and wanted to survive, made arrangements with Leech to pay him a regular tribute, a tax, and for that enjoyed "protection," both from the Leech Gang and the roving Mexican bandits. There were a few towns, though, that resisted. These he leveled, ruthlessly, and when the Governor of the State of Coahuila sent his personal army against Fort Leech, the ex-Missouri cavalryman leveled that, too.

For three years he took everything he wanted — their money, their food, their wine, their women — and withstood every effort to drive him out or capture him. The gang, however, changed personnel from time to time and for various reasons. Some got themselves killed, either by Mexicans or by a fellow bandit. Some grew weary of the hot, humid climate and crossed over into Texas and headed north. Some even fell out with Big Red and either just did get away or filled a fresh grave. Others, like the Perrott brothers and Sam Gill, left the gang for brief periods — leaves of absence — and went to raise hell elsewhere.

All this was known about Leech to the delegation of four merchants who had chartered a stage in Brownsville and were journeying to see him. They had gotten word to Fort Leech that they had a proposition for him and Leech, curious, not only guaranteed them safe entry and return but had them personally escorted across the Rio.

They were men of strength in their own right, these four. That they were still survivors of the jungle that was Brownsville proved that. But the nearer they got to Fort Leech the more their apprehensions grew, the more they doubted the wisdom of the long trip to this rattler's nest. Supposing he didn't accept their proposition and decided instead to hold them all for ransom. Ezra Owens could just see his partner back in Brownsville laughing uproariously at such a demand. Bert Bronsen thought about being held, too, but he was even more concerned about the tales of Leech's monumental drinking bouts, drunks that were reputed to last for weeks on end, and when the fog of whisky finally cleared there was carnage all around. Leech, it was said reliably, had personally killed a hundred men in the past three years. Even in Brownsville, Bronsen knew, life wasn't that cheap a commodity. Not even their legendary sheriff, John Lime, slaughtered in that style. The other two businessmen in the delegation, Ed Boone and Brad Hagood, told themselves they would be happy to be on their way back.

Then they were entering the converted mission itself, staring out at the up-to-date fortifications, the ready-looking array of cannons and U.S. Army-stolen equipment, and it was too late now to be worrying about being in the hands of Big Red Leech. The coach was driven into a courtyard, where a few men lounged in the shade, some still wearing remnants of the uniform they had fought the war in, but for every male present there were at least half a dozen girls in evidence — Mexican, Indian, even African — and the envoys wondered if Leech was experimenting along the lines of that Brigham Young fellow over in Utah.

A light-skinned, sloe-eyed Negress, in fact, opened the massive door to the main house to them, startling them with the uninhibited casualness of her bared torso. Nor could she be wearing much more below than the bright-flowered skirt, they decided, as the girl led them down the corridor. She stopped at a pair of double doors and knocked softly.

"Come on in!" a voice bellowed from the room beyond and she threw the doors open. Their first view of Red Leech made the descriptions of him seem pale and inadequate. From the place where his great booted feet were planted on the tile floor the red-bearded, green-eyed behemoth appeared to rise until it almost seemed that his great thatch of red hair brushed the ceiling. In one freckled fist he held a demijohn of wine by its throat, in the other a tortilla that had been baked to his own proportions. There were two other men in the room, mere six-foot, two-hundred pounders, and the same ratio and intermixture of females they had seen outdoors. In Matamoros, Bert Bronsen recalled strangely, there was an old recluse who kept cats. Scores and scores of cats. Cats wherever your glance happened to fall. Leech kept women. Every size and shape and coloring

52

— and each one naked to the waist.

"Help yourself, boys!" Leech roared, pointing with the tortilla to a marble-topped table containing more jugs, quarts of white corn and dark bourbon. "Help yourself to anything!" he added with ear-shattering hospitality, waving the tortilla around with nice indiscrimination at his assortment of women.

"I, ah, could do with a little drink," Ezra Owens said, crossing the threshold of the big, airy room. "Been a long, hot trip."

"You said it, brother! Well, come on in, boys! Nobody gonna eat you!" A wolfish grin parted the red beard. "Not yet!" he added, then laughed with a kind of uproarious ominousness. "We don't eat 'em, do we, Lash?" he asked one of his lazily reclining lieutenants.

"Sure don't, Big Red," Lash Wall answered. "Not till you give the word." As he spoke his sardonic gaze was on Bronsen, measuringly.

"We respect your word, Leech," the merchant said. "We know we'll come to no harm here."

"You said it, brother! Safe as church in Fort Leech!" Then he laughed again, disturbingly. "Which is just what it used to be!" he boomed. Leech ordered two of the girls to make drinks, which they served in sterling silver cups that had once graced a hacienda in San Carlos. The delegates from Brownsville took them, tried not to stare at the jutting breasts. All but Bronsen were regulars of Maude's on Harbor Street, men of the world, but there was a somewhat exotic difference about the nudity here that made them feel inadequate, shy as school-boys. Ed Boone couldn't shake the weird sensation that he had stepped from the stagecoach into a tale from the Arabian Nights.

"Comin' on siesta time!" Leech said in his powerful, blasting voice. "What's the deal — a bank?"

"A bank?" Bronsen repeated.

"That was the proposition down in Laredo," Leech said. "Jasper wanted me to rob the bank." He roared a laugh. "Sent Lash down to nose around. Y'know what? It was the damn jasper's own bank. He'd picked it clean and wanted me to pull his iron out of the fire."

"Did you?" Ezra Owens asked.

"Like hell, brother! But we touched the jasper up some. For how much, Lash?"

"Five thousand, seven hundred and fifty dollars," Lash answered boredly. "Heard later he hung himself."

"The wages of sin, boys! Is it a bank job?"

"Certainly not," Bronsen answered stiffly. "Every one of us has shares in the Bank of Brownsville. We built it from nothing . . ."

"Then you want the law took off your back?" Leech said. "Like we done two years ago up to Del Rio for the gamblers."

"I heard rumors about that," Ed Boone said hollowly. "Was that when you killed Sheriff Genova and his deputies?"

"For how much?" Leech asked his man.

"A thousand a man," Lash answered in the same indifferent voice.

"With satisfaction guaranteed, boys," Leech said, "or it don't cost a red cent. That your problem — too much law?"

"No," Bronsen said. "It's much bigger than that, Leech. Bigger stakes, I wager, than anything you've been offered."

"Then spill it, brother! This is when I siesta!"

"Could we, ah, have a little more privacy? It's hard to speak freely with such, ah, distractions."

"You said it, brother! Everybody vamnoose. Out!"

The girls and the other man left immediately. Lash Wall stayed as he was, sat a little straighter, perhaps, with the six-gun easier to get at. The visitors from Brownsville found seats for themselves and Bronsen began talking.

"What do you know about the Mexican trade, Leech?"

"That it's boomin' down your way, brother."

"Do you know any figures — say for the past two months?"

"Hell, that ain't my line!"

"One hundred thousand dollars," Bronsen said, "in cotton alone."

"Say, that's all right!" Leech said, exchanging a sly glance with Lash Wall that made Ezra Owens' heart skip a beat.

"No, Leech, it isn't all right at all," Bronsen told him. "Of that hundred thousand we realized less than half. The rest went to the Mexican officials — the governor, the politicians, the generals — every man who could get his hand in our pocket."

"Why, the dirty jackals!" Leech protested piously.

"Yes," Bronsen agreed, "and we've decided that it's high time we had a free trade over the border. We want to be able to ship our goods and make our fair profit."

"That's my motto, brother! Get your fair share every time. So what are you gonna do about it?"

"Our plan is twofold," Bronsen said. "First, we declare an embargo . . ."

"How's that?"

"We ship nothing at all across the river. Let's say for a period of sixty days. And then," Bronsen added, "we send everything across. For two weeks, day and night, we move our goods to our customers. That, Leech, is where you come in. We want to hire you and your men to convoy those goods."

Leech looked at the merchant, scowling. "For how much, brother?"

"For ten cents on every dollar received."

"Ten cents?" the outlaw roared. "What kind of piker you take Red Leech to be? Ten cents!"

"We plan to sell a million dollars worth," Bronsen replied quietly. "Your ten cents add up to one hundred thousand dollars."

The bright green eyes sparkled. "Well, brother, that's more like it!" He swung to Lash Wall. "How's that sound, boy?"

"We'll be working for our money, Big Red," the other one drawled. "And we're going to have to import a lot more gunslingers than we got at the fort now."

"How many men have you got here?" Bronsen asked.

"Seven, eight, ten," Leech said. "They come and go."

"Ten?" Bronsen echoed. "I was under the impression your band was much larger than that."

"What for?" Leech said. "Mister, you collect yourself four, five hundred Mex soldiers like the governor did a year back. Give me Lash here, and maybe two others. Then you come and try to move us out of my fort. You try!"

"But this operation's different, Big Red,"

Lash pointed out. "They want us to get their goods across the Rio. We'll be working two hundred miles from Fort Leech, out in the open."

Leech rubbed his beard. "Well, we'll send for boys then. Get me about thirty good ones."

"At least," Lash said.

"How long will it take to assemble them?"

"Hard to judge, brother. They're pretty spread out."

"A month?"

"Could be. Yeah, a month."

"And how long to get them to Brownsville?"

"Three, four days."

"Well, that ought to work into our plans perfectly," Bronsen said. "Do we have a deal?"

"A deal is what you got," Leech said, suddenly yawning. "See you in Brownsville."

The delegation left the room, climbed back into their stage and rode out of Fort Leech.

Big Red was already sprawled out on the oversized divan for siesta.

"Who all do you want to send for?" Lash asked.

"Make out a list. We'll go over it tonight."

"Sure thing."

"Be certain to put the Perrott brothers down. And Sam Gill."

"They were cuttin' up around Uvalde last I heard. Want me to start Pecos ridin' right now?"

"Anything you say, Lash. Only let me sleep till dark."

"Who gets to wake you?"

"Conchita, I think. Or Marie. Hell, I can't keep track."

"I'll tell 'em both, Big Red," the loyal Lash said.

"Yeah," Leech said sleepily. "Man don't want to play favorites."

That was a month ago, and during the next thirty days the word ranged far and wide that Big Red needed his boys in Brownsville. Something real special this time.

FOUR

BUCHANAN RODE INTO Beeville two hours after he left San Antone, went directly to the stable.

"I want this horse fed and watered," he said. "Have her ready to go in an hour." The liveryman shook his head.

"Got to wait your turn, fella."

"Not tonight," Buchanan said. "I'm on the move."

"On the prod, too, seems like."

"Yeh.

"After somebody?"

"Don't know yet. Listen, where do the freighters water their mules in this town?"

"There's a public trough outside a ways. But I sell 'em water, too."

"Remember anything of a new red wagon, six mules? Would have come through about a week ago."

"Sure do. Remember the wagon and the driver."

"Why do you remember him?"

"Never saw anybody so particular about getting mud off the wheels. Proud as a peacock over that wagon."

"He stay for the night?"

"Don't think so. He was pushin' it, just like you. Say, you ain't after that fella, are you?"

"Shouldn't I be?"

The man scratched his head. "Well, now you ask me, I don't know. Can't judge a book by the cover, so they say."

"He looked all right to you?"

"Yeah," the man said. "I kind of liked his looks."

Buchanan grinned. "Take my horse in her turn," he said. "Think I'll go have a steak."

"Have 'er ready in an hour," the man said, not to be outdone.

Buchanan went off to his dinner in considerably better spirits than the dark mood that had gripped him up in San Antone. Hell, he told himself, a lot of things could have gone wrong to delay old Rig. Lose a wheel, a sick mule, bad weather. Maybe he had trouble getting a full load for the return trip. Buchanan blamed himself, now, for attaching so blamed much importance to that eight days business. Since when, he demanded, are you such a Johnny-on-the-spot?

He ate leisurely, rode out of Beeville at a far easier and less determined pace than he'd ridden in. He was feeling so good, in fact, that he kept looking up the trail, half-expecting to see the Double-B Fast Freight rolling his way.

But he didn't see it. It was midnight when he reached Shelby, just the time when things seemed to be opening up in that rugged burg, and Buchanan entered the crowded lobby of the only hotel, shouldered his way to the desk.

"Full up, mister," the clerk told him and Buchanan got the curious notion that the dapper little man enjoyed delivering such a message.

"That's all right," he said. "Like to see the register, though."

"What for?"

"Looking for a friend that might be in town." He extended his hand for the open book but the clerk moved it aside.

"What's his name?"

"Bogan."

"Ain't here."

"You can tell without even looking?"

"Maybe it ain't worth my while to look."

Buchanan studied him more closely now, wondering what made people like this one tick. And wondering where he got his confidence from. He reached out again, not for the register this time but for the clerk himself. He took the man by his collar and was preparing to lift him bodily from behind the desk when there was interference from the rear. A gun barrel in his ribs and a gruff voice at his shoulder.

"Leggo of Henry," it said.

Buchanan didn't, but he paused to look into the tough face of the gunman. Or maybe not a gunman, unless that tarnished deputy badge on his shirt was a local joke. But there was whisky in him, and the click of the gun-hammer cocking was not funny at all.

"You gonna let Henry down?"

Buchanan did, not gently.

"That mouth of Henry's must keep you busy fulltime," he told the deputy.

"Just keep your own mouth shut up tight," was the surly, uneven reply.

"That's telling him, Jake," Henry said encouragingly.

"What's his beef, anyhow?" Jake asked the clerk.

"Just another damn troublemaker off the trail," Henry explained. "Thinks he's running things."

"You think you're running things?"

"I think if you don't pull that gun out of my ribs you're gonna eat it," Buchanan warned him. The deputy leered, shoved the barrel deeper. Buchanan's forearm dropped like a cleaver and his elbow clamped tight. The deputy grunted, dropped the forty-four to the wooden floor. Buchanan kicked it deftly away, and so far as he was concerned the incident should have ended right there.

Except that in brawl towns like Shelby

the law are wolves, they travel in packs, and the gunbutts that began crashing down on Buchanan's skull and neck and shoulders were being wielded by old hands at the game of gang-up. He sunk to his knees, groggy-eyed, and they still kept slashing at him. He fell over on his side and the one who smashed the toe of his boot into his face was Jake. Except that Buchanan was beyond caring.

He was brought to justice as soon as he was able to stand again and murmur his name through bloody lips. The trial was in the back room of a saloon, before a judge so drunk he could hardly keep his head up. The bailiff read the charges — disturbing the peace of Shelby, resisting lawful arrest and atrocious assault and battery. Jake was a witness and so was Henry, who turned out to be the sheriff's nephew. The case was open and shut and the judge handed down a unanimous verdict.

"Guilty," the bailiff explained. "A hundred dollars or a hundred days in the mine."

Naively, Buchanan reached for his money. It was gone, and now he remembered that he had ridden into Shelby with exactly the amount of the fine.

"You already paid, ranny. Now mount up and get the hell out of this town. We don't abide troublemakers."

Jake and two friends escorted him out of

the saloon, stood by like a trio of grinning apes as he climbed stiffly into his saddle. The night air seemed to clear Buchanan's head and he straightened his seat, made a slow turn with the horse. That brought him abreast of the three watchful deputies.

"Got some business south of here, boys," he said softly, managing a special smile of his own, a smile of anticipation. "But I'll be back one of these days. Count on it." He right-reined, all but brushed their faces with the filly's high rump and trotted out of Shelby with his quiet promise hanging in the night air.

Buchanan made his camp for the night just off the trail, arose with the dawn and pushed on. The traffic grew heavier as the new day got older, but none of the northbound freighters he questioned had knowledge of the Double-B wagon or its driver. These men, in fact, seemed to be without any knowledge of what might be coming along their back trail. Or were they evasive? Then it occurred to him that these were a lonely breed unto themselves, one for another, and that he probably looked like their common enemy: the man with the sheriff's order in his pocket, the lien on their wagons and their goods for a payment missed.

"The Double-*What* Fast Freight? Rig Who? Never heard of them, and I been hauling this route for ten years . . ."

But in Robstown there was freely given information about the bright red wagon, and in Bishop and Kingsville. Passed through a week or so ago. Remembered the color of the paint and the happy young cuss that drove her. Looked like he was sitting on top of the world in that seat.

No, he hadn't come back this way again. And today, Buchanan noted unhappily, would make the ninth day. Even if Bogan had been here in Kingsville this afternoon he had another two long days travel to reach San Antone.

A man don't tell his partner he'll be back in eight days when he isn't even going to make it in eleven. Or twelve. Or ever.

Buchanan, broke moneywise, busted in spirit, limped into Aura on a dragging, leg-weary horse. They were both also very hungry and he got off and walked her the length of Main Street to the stable.

"We need a meal," he told the owner. "I'll work for both of us."

The man, graying, in his sixties, peered through the darkening light at the face with its fresh bruises and old battlescars.

"Well, you're different, anyhow."

"Different?"

"You ain't swaggerin' in like you had the money then go off and deadbeat me for the feed and service."

"So how about it?"

"Ain't hardly enough this afternoon to buy my ownself supper. Especially since those three deadbeats came through town."

"You mean those stalls are all cleaned out?" Buchanan asked mildly. "The floor's soaped and hosed? Tomorrow's hay all forked and waiting for that big train I passed outside Kingsville?"

"How big a train?"

"Ten span, mister," Buchanan lied glibly. "Twenty mules that looked like they were accustomed to the best."

"Twenty head? Well!"

"Not to mention the damn carriages that clogged the trail out of Corpus Christi."

"Clogged?"

"One of those electioneering parties," Buchanan said. "Fella said it was Sam Houston campaigning for the Senate again. But I didn't see any sign of Houston myself."

"General Houston coming this way?"

"Not on my say-so," Buchanan said. "Though he could have been sleeping in that big gold coach in the middle. You've taken care of Sam's coach, haven't you?"

"Here? In this stable? I've sure heard about the General's coach, but I never had the honor of servicing it."

"Well, how about it, mister? You got enough work for two meals?"

"I sure have! Just lead that horse to the trough, son, and get busy on them dirty stalls. Soap and pail's over there in the corner somewhere. Give the floor a good wash. And don't forget tomorrow's hay. Better pitch it clear to the roof, all them mules comin'!"

He left the premises to Buchanan altogether, no doubt to spread the word about The Great God Houston, and as the teller of tall tales fell to with the manure shovel, the hard brush and the powerfully odorous lye soap he had good reason to suspect that he had overcooked his own goose.

But he saw to it that the filly got hers. She ate at the head of the table that evening, got bathed, curried and combed, a stall with a thick mattress of clean, fresh straw, a headway that faced west — so she wouldn't have the glare of the morning sun — and an ear-scratching to top it off.

After two hours his work was done — everything short of painting the stable — but when the owner still didn't return to pay him Buchanan's patience began to wear thin. As thin as his hunger was large. He wandered into the man's cluttered cubbyhole office and sat down in a sagging straw chair. On the desk was an invoice sheet bearing the name of the Aura Livery Co., Jason Hix, Owner, and Buchanan's glance went idly down the entries penciled onto it. One of the entries all but jumped up from the page.

"Double Freight," he read, "San Antonio. 6 mules. Feed P.M. & A.M. R. Bogan. $6 — Pd. in full."

There were three other entries grouped under the same date, a date just one week ago tonight, and reading the words again he realized that instead of being surprised that Rig had fed the animals and stayed overnight in Aura he should be reassured. For it meant that his partner was right on schedule so far as the southbound trip was concerned. He read the other names for that date. "Fred Perrott. Horse. Feed P.M. & A.M. $1 — Deadbeat."

Deadbeat, Buchanan thought. That's an ugly word. But right below was a second one, a Jules Perrott, and he had skipped town without paying a dollar. Father and son? Buchanan wondered. Brothers?

And a third deadbeat. Somebody named Sam Gill.

"Say, fella!" the liveryman's voice broke in, "you got this place looking just fine!"

Buchanan got up out of the chair.

"About given you up," he told him.

"Got into the blackjack game over to the saloon and lost track of the time. Sure some job you did here, though. How much do I owe you?"

"Whatever's the price of a meal in town," Buchanan said. "And I eat pretty hearty, too," he added.

69

"Imagine you do, furnace that size to stoke. Let's see now. You can get steak, spuds and pie at the saloon for a dollar. Probably want seconds on everything, won't you?"

"It's likely."

"Two dollars, then?"

"Fine.

"And one extra for good measure," Hix said, handing Buchanan three silver dollars.

"Two is fair," the tall man said. Hix smiled up at him.

"I won a little in the game," he said slyly. "In fact, the whole three dollars is on the dealer."

Buchanan accepted the coins. "See you lost three a week ago," he said.

"How's that?"

Buchanan glanced at the ledger. "The deadbeats," he said.

"Oh, them skunks. Not only cheat a man but get ornery about it." Hix looked at Buchanan sadly. "Liked to've had you here that morning," he said. "Wonder how hard they'd talk then."

"The fella with the mules paid, though," Buchanan said.

"On the barrelhead."

"You talk to him at all?"

"The night he drove in I did. Dished out the feed for his mules himself." Hix shook

his head. "Looked like regular donks to me,"
he said, "but he was real particular. And
that red wagon! Why, he spent one solid
hour out back just scrubbing that thing till
it shined like new." The remembering made
the old man chuckle. "I joshed him some
about that, told him he acted like it was all
paid for."

"What did he say to that?"

"He said no, there was a long ways to go
yet. But he said it was going to be paid for,
and then he was going to get another, just
like it. Sure had the vinegar in him, that
one."

"But you haven't seen him since?"

"No," Hix said, his face becoming puzzled.
"What is it?"

"You ask me if I've seen that driver and
it reminds me that he should have been
back from Matamoros three, four nights
ago. Least, that's what he planned. Said
this was his lucky town."

"Lucky?" Buchanan repeated. "What did
he mean?"

"Don't rightly know," Hix said, then
smiled. "But he did take a real shine to
Cristy."

"Who?"

"Cristina, the pretty gal that deals the
games over at the saloon. Everybody calls
her Cristy," Hix said, "and I guess just
about everybody off the trail shines up to

her. Just like the fella we're talking about. Say, do you know him?"

"I'm his partner," Buchanan said.

"Why, sure!" Hix said. "Sure you are! Ten feet tall he said you was and ate wildcat raw for breakfast." The man laughed. "I think he even put you up a notch over that red wagon and them six mules." The smile faded. "Ain't nothing gone wrong, is there?"

"That's what I came down the trail to find out," Buchanan said. "Right at the moment, though, I'm going to hunt up that steak you mentioned." He went out of the stable and moved up Main Street. On the corner was the saloon, just that — SALOON — and he went inside.

Went in expecting no surprises and getting none, for if Buchanan had seen this place once in his travels he had seen it a hundred times. A bar against the wall with men hunched over their beers and their whiskies. Tables with older drinkers, men who spoke occasionally to their comrades but for the most part just sat and stared into space, lost in some reverie of the past, some memory of a missed chance. And another table, larger than the rest and better lighted, where the nightly game was played. Blackjack, Hix had said, but the four men sitting around it now were dealing stud. And there was no Cristy, "the pretty gal that deals the games."

Well, Buchanan wasn't going to shine up to her. But he damn well intended to find out what Rig meant by calling this his lucky town. Buchanan figured that one look would tell him if Bogan had found himself a second Ruthie Stell, if he was so delayed getting back because he was selling Magee's cotton on his own and their wagon along with it. One look would tell him that, and then a few hard questions to find out what their plans were, where she figured to join him.

There was a stairway in the back of this saloon, nothing as wide and fancy as Queenie's, but it led directly to a room and the door to that room was shut tight.

"I'd like the steak and potatoes," Buchanan told the bartender, a fellow about his own thirty years and clean shaven. "Not too done." The order was relayed to a Chinaman in the kitchen.

"Drink while you're waiting?"

"How much is the bourbon?"

"Two bits."

"And how big is the steak?"

"One pound."

Buchanan frowned, deliberating between his keen thirst and his voracious hunger. The bartender waited patiently, almost sympathetically.

"A double bourbon," Buchanan said. The drink was poured in an outsize glass and

Buchanan looked his thanks. "Better not let the boss catch you," he said good-naturedly and the barkeep smiled.

"I'm the boss," he said.

"In that case I'm twice obliged, friend. Where do you want me to eat that steak?"

"Any table that suits you."

Buchanan took the drink to one in the rear, sat down in almost complete darkness. The cook brought the steak out within minutes, stood by during the first cut to see if it was too rare. Buchanan's big grin assured him.

"You don't fool me," the big man said.

"Please?"

"You're no restaurant cookie. You worked on a ranch."

"That right, that right. But better here now. Sleep every morning way past dawn. You own big ranch?"

"Not quite yet," Buchanan admitted, taking another cut of meat.

"But by-an'-by," the cook said.

"Oh, sure."

"Big, big ranch. Fifty thousand acre."

"At least."

"Hundred thousand cattle."

"Thereabouts."

"You want other steak now?"

Buchanan suddenly broke into laughter. "No," he said, enjoying the joke on himself. "Can't afford another steak."

The Chinaman laughed along with him. "You still get big ranch," he said and retreated to his kitchen. Buchanan went on with his meal, was draining the last of the strong black coffee when the door at the head of the stairs opened and a girl stepped from the room beyond. Just before she closed the door again he had a glimpse of a bedstead, a table with a pitcher and wash bowl on it, and through Buchanan's mind passed the half-melancholy, half-unpleasant picture of the faceless man still lying there, passed out drunk.

He looked at her now, watched her descend the rather steep stairs, and reminded himself that he was going to need but one look to tell him the answer about herself and Rig Bogan.

Well, he hedged now, she sure wasn't another Ruthie Stell. Not physically, at any rate. This time Rig had gone for the tall, blonde type, with a pale and expressionless face that was like a beautiful mask. A complete change-about from Ruthie Stell, Buchanan conceded, but what man wouldn't try to change his luck after the way that affair had worked out?

Now she was at the bottom of the stairs, turning right and walking toward the card table, and Buchanan had used up that one look by a long margin as he studied the interesting motion of her lithe body beneath

75

the well fitting, short-skirted dress. Who, he asked himself, did she remind him of? And just as she was being seated at the table he remembered.

This girl looked and walked like a woman he had seen in San Francisco. An actress named Roxanne something-or-other. He had seen her twice. Once on the stage, as the heroine of the stupidest play that was ever written. And seen her again the very next night, entering a restaurant on the arm of Dan P. White, the richest man in California. She'd gone on a trip around the world with him, Buchanan had heard, and that was two long years ago. Funny he should have remembered that particular face and that particular walk after all this time.

A gun went off somewhere up the street. A second one, a third, probably a dozen shots in all, and Buchanan was somewhat surprised at the frightened reaction they caused here in this saloon. Couldn't they tell the sound of a .45 being fired into the air? The men at the bar had all swung around to face the swinging doors. The players at the table all held their cards as if frozen. Even the mask-like face of the girl dealer showed emotion — and it was fear. As he watched she turned her head toward the bar and Buchanan caught the anxious glance that she exchanged with the bartender.

Well, that's East Texas for you, he thought. Last night, up in Shelby, gunfire was as natural a sound as barking dogs. A couple of miles further south and the citizens act like they never heard a gun.

The swinging doors opened with a bang and three burly, hard-faced men came through single file, stopped when they were inside and stood shoulder to shoulder, thumbs hooked into their belts. Each pair of eyes looked around the room but it was as though it were one man.

"Any law on the premises?" the hardcase in the middle asked and Buchanan, as he always did, tried to place the speaker's region. A twangy-sounding voice that bit the words off sharp. Missouri, he guessed. Or maybe Kansas.

"Sheriff Rivercomb is laid up," someone at the bar answered meekly, and that made the Missourian, or Kansan, laugh.

"Wynt," he said too loudly to the man on his right, "did you go and send word we was comin'?"

"Christ, no, I didn't!" Wynt answered. "You know, Prado, how I like to make these Texas sheriffs jig!"

Missouri, definitely, Buchanan decided, and made himself a little bet on the side that they hadn't come through Shelby with big talk like that.

Now they were walking toward the bar,

single file again like ex-soldiers, Buchanan noted, and half a dozen men quickly gave away their places to them.

"Put the bottle on the bar and take your ugly face away," Prado told the bartender. Buchanan straightened up in his chair, his broad face expectant, pantherish. He liked this bartender, felt indebted to him for the extra measure of bourbon. Now he waited for the fellow to give these loudmouths the word — and take his own hand in the fun that would follow.

Instead, the bottle was produced and his new friend faded to the other end of the bar. Buchanan sat back, frowning. At the next table an old man was speaking to his companion, his voice a low, protesting undertone.

"What in the tarnation's goin' on around here, anyhow?" he demanded.

"Shh, Charlie! Keep your voice down!" the other one cautioned in a whisper.

"That's what I mean, dagnabit! For the last two weeks now a person can't hardly draw a free breath in this town! A regular damn parade of these hardcase bullies . . ."

"Shh, Charlie! You want them to come back here?"

"But where they comin' from? Where they goin'? Why do they have to stop in Aura? Look at them standin' there, starin' around like they was the three cocks-of-the-walk and us decent folks was dirt. Just look at their mean faces, Rob . . ."

"Charlie, you're gonna get us gunwhipped just like poor old John Rivercomb."

"Well, at least John stood up to them two Perrotts, or whatever their names was."

"John is paid to stand up to trouble-makers," Rob whispered back. "He asked to get elected and that's part of the job."

The man named Charlie had chanced to look over his shoulder and spot the huge, somehow formidable figure looming in the semi-darkness above the other table. He turned his head quickly, mumbled something behind his hand to Rob. Rob stiffened in fear, and it was Buchanan's impulse to get up and join them, reassure them about his own peaceful intentions. He pushed his chair back, started to rise, when the voice of the one called Prado took his and every-one else's attention.

"Well, will you looka there, boys!" he shouted nasally, his voice breaking over the other strained, hesitant sounds in the room, his beady-eyed glance directed to-ward the girl dealing blackjack. Now the silence was complete and every head swung to that table. Including Buchanan, who marked that she blinked her eyes once, then regained her cool composure in the next moment. She looked over the cards of the four players betting against her, made her decision and turned up the hole card.

"King, six," she announced in a clear, professional tone. "Pay seventeen!" Two of her opponents collected, two lost.

She knows the odds, Buchanan thought, and then that annoying voice sounded off from the bar again.

"Pay seventeen!" Prado called over to her in a kind of churlish mockery. "Girlie, I pay eighteen. Whatta you say?"

"Nineteen!" his friend Wynt offered. "What's your bid, Sherm?" he asked the third one.

"For that blonde?" Sherm said. "Twenty-five dollars."

Prado took two steps forward from the bar, swung around to face them.

"Who asked her first?" he said.

"You did, Prado," Wynt said.

"Then wait your goddamn turn!"

"Sure, Prado, sure. You, then me, then Sherm."

"Then Big Red," Sherm said and that made them all burst out in raucous laughter.

"After us comes Big Red!" Prado bawled. "We'll take her down for a present!" More laughter.

"Well, let's go, let's go," Wynt said eagerly. Prado turned, stood again with thumbs hooked inside his belt. His gaze was leveled insolently at the girl's profile and now she gave up the pretense of dealing, swung her head to face him.

"Come on over here," Prado ordered. She said nothing, sat motionless, but a sudden rise of her breasts betrayed her fear to every man in the room. "I said to come over here," Prado said again.

Wynt laughed, goadingly. "You ain't doin' so hot, Prado," he taunted.

"We'll see, by damn!" He started forward, his bullneck bowed.

"Leave her be!" the bartender shouted raggedly and in his hands was a double-barrelled shotgun. The man's face was white and the weapon trembled uncontrollably in his grasp. Prado had stopped and now he looked back over his shoulder.

"Get out!" the barman said wildly. "Get out of here, the three of you!"

"Sure," Prado said, his own voice ominously controlled. "We'll get out if you say so." As he spoke he began a sidling movement to his left. The shotgun barrel swung with him, as if drawn by a magnet, kept swinging until the barman could no longer observe Wynt. That one's hairy hand reached out for the bottle, furtively. His fingers wrapped themselves around the neck.

"We'll get out," Prado was still saying. "We'll do whatever you say, buddy."

Several things happened then, so closely

spaced they seemed all of one piece.

Wynt's arm flashed overhead, the bottle held like a club.

The girl tried to scream a warning.

From the dark corner in the back of the room a Colt .45 jumped and roared. Wynt was suddenly holding nothing over his head but his fist, which he stared at wonderingly.

Things continued to happen. The bartender whirled around and Prado closed in, tore the shotgun loose from his grip and flung it aside. Now he gave his full attention to the tall figure looming above the table in the corner.

"Fan out, boys!" he snapped, taking a backward step himself, his body in a tight crouch, his gaze as unwavering as a cobra's. Sherm moved away from him, further down the bar. Wynt glided in the opposite direction and now they had their opponent ringed with a wall at his back.

Slick crew, Buchanan thought, revising his estimate of Missouri gunfighters upwards.

The Colt's thundering voice demolished the silence and its big slug took Prado squarely in the middle, slammed him to his knees.

Well, don't look at me like that, brother. You called this tune and now you pay the fiddler.

"Jesus!" Wynt yelled piercingly and Buchanan gave it to him up high, at the collarbone. Wynt turned with his wound and stumbled like a drunken man toward the street, his simple mind unable to cope with the swift and bewildering turn of events.

Buchanan holstered the busy Colt, took two leisurely steps into the brighter light.

"You," he said to Sherm, "get to draw. Let's go."

Sherm filled his barrel chest with a deep breath, licked his dry lips.

"Some other time, brother," he said hollowly. "You're a little too anxious."

"Then pick up the ladies' man and be on your way."

Sherm glanced briefly at the unmoving Prado. "He looks dead to me," he said.

"Bury him then."

Sherm obviously didn't like that, but the alternative had even less appeal. He got Prado under the armpits, dragged him unceremoniously across the saloon floor, through the doors. They swung back and forth on their leather hinges and the soft creaking seemed to be the last sound left in the world. And then Buchanan's heels clicked on the boards as he walked toward the bar. The tall man fished into his pocket, brought out two of his three hard-earned silver dollars and set them down. The barkeep stared at the money then raised his eyes to Buchanan's face. He looked to be in a state of shock.

"What," he asked, "is that for?"

"Double bourbon and a steak dinner. Damn fine cook you got, too. Hang on to him."

The laughter started deep in the bartender's stomach, came bubbling up and overflowed as a geyser of joyous relief. Came from him and was echoed by the next man, the next, spread through that room like nothing else but a prairie fire. Buchanan gazed around at them, heard his simple statement repeated in gleeful tones, and told himself a second time tonight that East Texans were a curious breed.

Now a perfect stranger had hold of his hand and was pumping it like he was trying to raise water. His back was being whacked with great gusto, his forearms squeezed, and into his ears poured a torrent of praise that was not only damn foolish but plain embarrassing. Hell's holy bells, in this town they'd give you a medal for shooting fish in a barrel.

There was a hand suddenly resting in his huge palm that was neither calloused nor broad nor sweating. It was smooth and slim and coolly impersonal. Buchanan looked down, but not too far, into a pair of coppery-brown, frankly appraising eyes. The blonde Rig Bogan had taken a shine to. That everyone off the trail took a shine to. Including the recently departed Prado.

Their meeting seemed to cause a hush over the crowd. The other voices trailed away.

"I want to thank you for helping my brother," she said, with a certain emphasis on the word brother, Buchanan thought, to make it crystal clear that she'd needed no particular help for herself. She could have handled Prado, Wynt, Sherm and the entire male species. With a well placed word, no doubt. Then she smiled, revealing rows of teeth that were as white and strong-looking as high-polished ivory. "And I'm sure," she added, "that the drink and the dinner are on the house."

The cool hand was withdrawn. The audience with the queen of Aura was concluded. But Buchanan, apparently, hadn't been dazzled in the fashion to which she was accustomed for she paused for an extra moment.

"Is there something wrong?" she asked.

"I want to have a talk with you," he said. Her eyelids went down, like a shade, and when they opened again the eyes were ten degrees colder.

"About Rig," Buchanan said.

"Who?"

"Rig Bogan." He gave her a sudden, violent

shove away from him, one brief instant before the gun aimed at them above the doors blazed its vicious fury. Shoved the girl and ducked low himself as the assassin outside kept firing.

Buchanan cleared the Colt, aimed guessingly at the top of the door and threw out a reply. A second and a third. Then the hammer clicked once on the empty casing that had blown the bottle out of Wynt's fist, again on the one that had taken Prado to eternity.

But the three live slugs had driven the sniper's gun to cover and the silence now was golden. Buchanan's eye fell on the discarded shotgun nearby. He cradled it in his hands and moved swiftly toward the doors, shouldered one of them open and stepped into the street. Fifty yards to the south a single rider was running away, a man whose body tilted curiously in the saddle. Wynt, Buchanan guessed, who had to favor that busted collarbone. The shotgun might carry to him, but what the hell?

He turned, instead, and re-entered the saloon, laid the rifle atop the bar and made his way to where the girl was seated after being helped from her rude fall.

"You all right?"

She nodded her head, managed a smile. "You move quickly when you have to," she said.

"Didn't mean to shove that hard. What's the matter?"

One moment she was staring at his middle and the next she had sprung to her feet. "You're wounded," she told him. "You're bleeding!"

He looked down at the wet stain just above his gunbelt. "Well I'll be damned," he said, smiling ruefully, as if he had committed something rather foolish. She had him by the arm and was turning him around.

"Come upstairs," she said.

"What for?"

"So you can get off your feet. Mr. Price, would you ride out to Doc's house right away?"

"You betcha!"

"Come on," she said to Buchanan. "Up these stairs."

He held back, remembering. "This isn't anything," he assured her.

"How do you know?" she said with the kind of anger you use for a child.

"After a while," Buchanan explained, "you get to tell between a little scratch and a hole. This is a scratch."

"We'll let Doc Vincent decide that," she told him firmly. "Until then you're going to lie down."

"Might as well do what Cristy says," said her bartender brother. "She'll save your life if she has to hound you to death."

"That's very funny, Steve," she replied, pulling Buchanan insistently toward the staircase.

"How about the other gent?" he asked in an undertone.

"What other gent?"

"Isn't there somebody up there?"

Her eyebrows shot skyward. "Up there?" she said. "In my room? What would a man be doing in my room?"

Buchanan winced. "I just thought . . . I mean, I . . ."

"Well, you can just think again!"

"Miss, I'm sorry," Buchanan apologized. "I really am."

"Let's stop talking and get you quiet until the doc gets here," she said with finality, urging him up the steps. He went along now, not daring to protest after making such a jackass of himself.

Not that he didn't have a few questions about Rig Bogan, though. The only difference was, he wouldn't put them to her quite so bluntly now. He had been only briefly singed by her anger a moment ago and he was sure he didn't want the full treatment.

She opened the door, stood aside for him to pass on through. It was a small room with a single window, big enough to accommodate only an armchair and a table in addition to the washstand and the single bed. The empty single bed with the crisp white sheet and pillowcase, the light blue blanket.

"Well, at least my gent made the bed before he sneaked out through the window," she commented.

"I said I was sorry, ma'am."

"Sorry because you were wrong? Take your shirt off and lie down."

"Just sorry," he said. "And I'm not going to mess that bed."

"You can be stubborn, can't you?"

"Only when I'm pushed," he said and that made her pause, give his rugged face a close study.

"Yes," she said, less brusquely. "And you've been pushed." She reached up, began unbuttoning the shirt herself.

"I can do that."

"You take the gunbelt off."

Buchanan did the one, she the other. After she peeled the shirt from his shoulders he went and laid the gunrig across the back of the chair.

"Horrible," he heard her say and turned his head.

"Me?"

"The gun. All guns."

He smiled at her. "It started with fists," he said. "Then clubs and spears. Now we got guns."

"And men who get paid to use them . . ." Her voice broke off. "I imagine that includes you," she said and Buchanan laughed.

"Earned me a drink and dinner tonight," he said.

She smiled back. "And that little scratch the whole length of your side," she said, coming toward him with a towel in her hand. She laid the towel over the gash, pressed gently. "Another inch," she said, "and there'd be a bullet in your body."

"It's a life of inches."

"It's a life of . . . You'd better lie down," she said. "Hold the towel close and maybe the bleeding will stop a little."

Buchanan did as he was told. He stretched out and his legs extended the bed by six inches.

"Lordy," she laughed, "how tall are you, anyhow?"

"Too damn, sometimes." He turned his shaggy head sideways and sniffed suspiciously.

"What's the matter?"

"Perfume in the pillow," he said. "That's a new one on me."

"Not where I come from."

"Carolina," Buchanan said. "Or Tennessee."

"South Carolina. But how did you know?"

"My favorite pastime. Placing people by their voices."

"Is this the patient?" an old man asked from

the doorway and came inside the little room. "Good gravy," Doc Vincent said, his lively eyes traveling the length of Buchanan. "Ought to charge you by the square foot."

"Better keep the bill under three dollars, Doc," Buchanan said.

"That's been taken care of," he said, leaning down and pulling the towel away. He spent the next five minutes cleaning the wound and bandaging it. "Better stay off your feet for a couple of days. Give it a chance to scab."

"You bet, Doc. Much obliged."

"Glad I could help. 'Night, mister. 'Night, Cristine." He went out, and as soon as the door closed Buchanan was swinging his legs to the floor.

"What do you think you're doing?" she demanded.

He stood up, reached out for his shirt. Her hand got to it first, snatched it behind her back.

"You," she said, "are going to lie down, and I'm going to wash this shirt. And take that stubborn look off your face."

Buchanan looked down at her for a long moment.

"Let's have that talk about Rig Bogan," he said.

"You mentioned him before," she said. "Is he the fellow who drove the red wagon through town last week?"

"That all you know about him?"

"Yes," she said. "That's all I know about any fellow who comes through."

"He told the liveryman this was his lucky town. He thinks he means on account of you're here."

She began to shake her head puzzledly. Then her face brightened. "He means the game that night he was here," she said. "And I'll say he was lucky. He broke the bank and everyone else playing." She smiled. "Sat there grinning and turning up blackjack three times out of every five."

"How much did he win?"

"Well, there was a hundred in the bank. That's my limit and he won it all. And he must have taken those three toughs for another hundred apiece."

"What toughs?"

"Three just like the ones that came in tonight. Two of them were brothers."

"And Rig busted them?"

She nodded. "Then he left. That was when they started drinking and turned surly. Poor Sheriff Rivercomb tried to quiet them and they beat him with their guns."

"They bother you?"

"I got out and drove to my brother's house. Why all these questions?"

"I'm looking for Rig Bogan," Buchanan

said. "We're partners in that red wagon he was driving."

"So you're the famous partner," she said. "Every time he'd win a pot he'd say, 'Boy, if only old Buchanan could see me now!' I thought he'd drive me crazy."

"I wish old Buchanan could see him now."

"Is something wrong?"

He told her what was wrong. Even told her about his suspicions concerning Bogan and herself.

"You came in here tonight with a lot of ideas about me," she said.

"All of them wrong."

"But intriguing, though," she said with a sad smile. "More intriguing than this existence."

"You don't like what you're doing?"

"*Like* it? I hate every minute of it."

"How'd you come to leave Carolina?"

She took a deep breath, walked over to the window. "My husband was killed in a duel," she said very quietly. "It was all very gallant."

"What was the duel about?"

"It seems that another gentleman made a remark about me, about my — virtue — before David married me. David challenged him to a duel and this other man put a bullet in his heart." She swung around. "That's why all guns are horrible," she said.

"A man," Buchanan said, "sees it different

93

from a woman. Me, I don't know what else your husband could have done."

"David's mother says I could have stopped him."

"How?"

She looked across the dimly lit room steadily. Beneath the bodice of the dress her breasts rose and fell emotionally.

"David's mother said I should have told him that what the man had said about me was the truth," she said slowly. "She pointed out that we'd only been married a month, that we really hadn't formed any deep attachment. I should have sacrificed our marriage, his mother said, to save his life."

"That lady was wrong," Buchanan said.

The blonde girl's head came up in surprise. "You think so? You really think she was wrong?"

"She'd have been wrong if you were my wife," Buchanan answered her. "I'd have looked up this jasper regardless."

The smile that came to her lips seemed grateful. "For some reason you make me feel better," she told him. "As if I couldn't have changed anything that happened. Thank you." She came away from the window, still holding his shirt. "I'm going to take this down to the kitchen and wash it out," she said. "At least lie down for that little time."

"All right."

She went past him and out of the room. Buchanan looked down at the bed thoughtfully, unable for the moment not to think of the little story he had just been told. A marriage that had lasted one brief month. He had a picture in his mind of a beautiful young bride riding in an open carriage with a handsome, smiling young fellow who cut a dashing figure in a long jacket and rakish beaver hat. Then some drunk at a bar has to open his dirty mouth. Buchanan could even imagine him as a beau who had lost out. She must have had beaux like a flame has moths. And the sonofabitch was probably a dead shot with one of those tricky duelling pistols. It would be one of those strictly formal affairs, at dawn, with everybody being so goddamn polite to each other. "Take six paces, gentlemen, then turn and fire." A wedding and a funeral in one short month.

And this lonely bed in this little room.

Buchanan lay down on it again, smelling the perfume in the pillow, staring at the crack in the ceiling just as she must stare at it one long night after another.

Bogan. Think about Rig. Stop looking at the ceiling. Bogan, he told himself again. Bogan winning money from what she called "those three toughs." What was the name in the ledger — Perrott? Two brothers named Fred and Jules Perrott. And a third man named Sam Gill. They'd lost their money and turned surly, taken it out on some old sheriff. And topped off their stay by running out on a lousy one-dollar feed bill.

What was he trying to remember now? A conversation. The codger at the table downstairs had wondered at the steady parade of noisy guns through town. Some recruiting going on around here? Somebody stirring the pot?

Lost a hundred dollars apiece, she'd said. Lost it to a grinning freighter who probably wasn't even packing a gun. Had the brothers and their friend ridden south that morning, the same direction as Rig?

Buchanan closed his eyes. His great hands folded slowly into fists, unfolded again and lay still beside him. He should be on the trail himself. Right now. He smothered a yawn. Tomorrow he'd be riding, all day, south to Brownsville and Matamoros.

Buchanan closed his eyes, and when he opened them again there was a faint gray light coming into the room beneath the drawn shade. It was coming on dawn and he had slept the hours away in her bed. But then he recalled her mentioning her brother's house and he felt a little better. Until he turned his head and found her curled up in the chair, and then he felt terrible.

And worse when he realized that the blanket had been thrown over him, that his boots had been removed. Him the ranny that slept with one eye open and both ears cocked, that could hear a rattler sigh at three hundred feet.

His shirt, washed and ironed, hung above the door. Oh, Buchanan, you horse's ass! he growled at himself. What a performance! He came out of the bed scowling, let go with a self-disgusted sigh, then walked softly in his stockinged feet to where she slept, looking somehow both cramped and comfortable with her knees drawn up against her chest, her head pillowed on her forearm.

Easy, now, he cautioned, bending over the chair, lifting her effortlessly in his arms and settling her into the bed. Now he returned the favor, covered her to the chin with the blanket, went and got the fresh-smelling shirt and put it on. He picked up the boots from the floor, carried them out of the room and on down the stairs. Buchanan left the saloon via the kitchen door, walked back down Main Street to the stable.

This, he reflected, would have been about

the time that Rig would have departed Aura seven mornings ago. The other three would have slept off their drunk till mid-morning, ridden out of town at a defiant, hungover gallop.

FIVE

THE COUNTRY SOUTH of Aura was stark and rugged, sparsely settled, and Buchanan traveled through it at a pace that was deceptively casual. He was trying to put himself in Rig Bogan's place a week ago, to think the other man's thoughts as he hit the trail again after a pleasant night of leisure and winning at cards. I'd be feeling pretty good about now, Buchanan mused. That money I won would have a comforting feel inside my shirt and I'd be telling those mules that it took some talent to break the bank at blackjack.

But would I give a thought to my back-trail? Buchanan wondered. Every so often would I give a look over my shoulder to see if I was having company along this lonely stretch? Buchanan glanced back himself, saw nothing but empty flatland, and decided that even a man half-cautious would be hard to surprise here.

But within the hour the terrain changed, became hilly, and a few miles further south there was a junction in the trail. A rider had a choice of turning almost due east along level ground or ascending a long, sharp incline if he was determined to continue south. What did a freight driver do here? What was Rig's choice? Did the flat trail eventually work its way southward again? Did the route up the face of this small mountain lose a man time or gain it?

Me, Buchanan decided, I'd take the hills as they came, provided I was still headed in the right direction. He put the undaunted filly to the steep climb. When he reached the top, though, he wasn't so sure. The trail up here was narrower, hemmed in by heavy brush, and didn't look as used as the one below. He followed it slowly, his mind nagged by the certainty that he would eventually have to turn back, start all over again down at the junction. Twenty minutes later he reined in, started to swing the animal around, when the blazing morning sun caught the patch of bright red paint and made it glisten in his eye.

Buchanan kneed the horse to the edge of the trail, peered straight down. There, lying on its side at the bottom of the gorge, was the forlorn wreckage of the wagon. The words DOUBLE-B FAST FREIGHT appeared to mock Buchanan's gaze. He dismounted, started to work his way down the steep, jagged side, hoping against hope that there was no more to the story than the toppled wagon. But there was more. Rig

Bogan's lifeless, bullet-riddled body lay fifty feet from his beloved red wagon, half-hidden by the jutting boulder that had arrested his plunge from the trail above, and Buchanan's examination of it was expressionless, unemotional. Six times he had been shot, from the back of the head to the base of the spine, and it was not likely, Buchanan thought, that he had lived long enough to even realize what had happened to him.

A deep, pent-up sigh escaped the tall man's cavernous chest and he turned away from his murdered partner, walked slowly to the ruins of their venture. The mules had been freed from their harness before the wagon was sent plunging into the gorge and Buchanan reflected briefly on the nice difference the bushwhackers placed on animal life and human. Nor had they considered Honest John Magee's cotton to be worth much. A few bales of the shipment still lay in the truck, the rest were scattered over the ground. Scattered, too, was the odd cargo that Rig had scouted up in San Antone and taken on consignment. As Buchanan retrieved a shiny new shovel he could hear Rig's eager voice again, making the deal with the shipper, assuring the man of safe delivery and a good profit.

He carried the shovel to a secluded, semi-shaded spot near the wall of the canyon and began the hard, unhappy chore of digging a decent resting place. The rocky ground yielded very slowly and the sun was in the middle of the cloudless sky before the grave was ready. Buchanan laid Rig Bogan into it with a tarpaulin for a shroud. He picked up a shovelful of dirt.

"Fred Perrott," he said aloud and poured the dirt back into the grave. "Jules Perrott," he said with the second shovelful. "And Sam Gill," he said with the third, passing judgment equally on all three. It was spoken tonelessly, matter-of-factly, and had anyone heard the deep voice they would have known there was no appeal from the sentence.

Buchanan finished his work quickly, as if anxious to be gone, and walked away from the grave without a backward glance. But as he was starting to climb the gorge again he glanced up to find a mounted figure watching him from the trail. It was the girl, Cristy, and how long she had been there Buchanan neither wondered nor cared. When he reached the top again he noted that she was dressed in levis and a shirt, that the blue blanket from her bed was now rolled behind her saddle. He went to his own horse, threw a leg up.

"Was that your partner down there?" Cristy asked him.

"The big winner," Buchanan said. She studied him, marked the cold detachment of his voice and manner.

"It wasn't — an accident?" she asked.

Buchanan shook his head curtly. "They didn't give him a chance," he said, and started off.

"Wait!" she called out, impulsively.

He looked around. "I did my waiting back in San Antone," he said.

"But where are you going now? What are you going to do?"

His smile was bleak and cheerless. "Going to collect some damages," he said.

"Do you know where they went?"

"I'm betting they continued south."

She had ridden up to him. Now her eyes were full on his face. "Can I go along," she asked, "as far as Brownsville?"

Buchanan frowned, then shrugged. "Why not?" he replied.

"Thank you," she said and that reminded him.

"Thank you for the use of your bed last night," he told her. "And the clean shirt."

She colored slightly, smiled at him. "I was — surprised to find you gone," she said, choosing that word at the last moment.

"Yeh," Buchanan said, cutting off any further conversation. "Well, let's ride." He took off abruptly, at a restless trot, and she was some seconds in following. This, Cristy thought, is a different man than the warm and easygoing one she had felt so comfortable with last night. She could remember how he looked when she'd come back to the room and found him so peacefully sleeping, how she'd sat in the chair and been content to observe him in repose for the better part of an hour. Gaze at him and know that for all the strong and proud and fiercely independent men who came in off the trail this one here was what the Mexicans meant by *un hombre todo*. All man — and, for now, within the four walls of her small room, all hers. Other women who had thought the same? Oh, yes. The battered nose and the crescent scar on his cheekbone had come from men. But the gentle curve at the end of his lips, the smile in his eyes, the caressing tone of his voice — those had been gifts from beautiful women.

She could remember the sharp sense of loss to awake this morning and find him gone. The impulse that had seized her to follow after him, to go wherever he went . . .

But he was changed now. He was hard and withdrawn, cold and aloof on the outside but consumed by a fire that raged in his mind and his heart. His partner had been killed and robbed. He was going to avenge that even at the cost of his own life. And there was no place in those grim plans for a woman and her feminine ways. She knew that and rode on behind him, keeping silent.

Six

THE WILDEST OF the wild towns on the border of the Rio Grande was Brownsville. There were five thousand people living there, mostly Mexican, but it was the Americans and French who raised all the hell. Escaped criminals headed for Brownsville — thieves, murderers, rapists — as if it were second nature. So did the deserters from the army, and discredited gamblers, and swindlers, and scores of other men whose souls were bankrupt. And their women. Women who belonged to everybody and anybody.

This is not to say there wasn't law in Brownsville. There was. His name was John Lime. Sheriff Lime had been a captain with the famous Doniphan Raiders during the war, a slim, medium-sized man possessed of outsized personal courage, and though a lot of men wondered how Lime perpetuated himself in office, or how he had come to power in the first place, there were very, very few who had ever asked out loud and lived to hear an answer.

Sheriff Lime, who was forty years old,

considered Brownsville as his personal pre-serve and dispensed his justice on a per-sonal level — without wasting time on juries and judges. Or jails. Oh, Brownsville owned a jail — a doorless, open-air adobe building whose guards were a trio of vicious mastiffs — but John Lime considered confinement a waste of effort except in special cases. A serious crime, such as out-and-out mur-der, cheating at cards, armed robbery of a merchant or the bank, was punishable by hanging over in Shantytown. Lesser crimi-nals were simply run out of town by Lime's tough, well-disciplined band of deputies.

John Lime enjoyed dispensing the law for its own sake, but there were other compen-sations. There were in Brownsville, for in-stance, a total of fifty gambling houses, saloons and bordellos, and the sheriff was a full partner in every one. He also partici-pated in both the toll bridge across the river to Matamoros and the ferryboat. Nor did a single steamboat tie up at a Brownsville wharf without paying tribute, in the form of a daily permit, to the sheriff's office. His income was considerable, and John Lime was a wealthy man.

But he did like his job and the power, and he did take a proprietary interest in Brownsville — which might just as well have been called Limesville or Johnstown — and when Bert Bronsen and Ezra Owens first thought of their scheme to run contraband cargo past the Mexican customs they were careful to bring it to John Lime for his approval. The sheriff heard them out with a thoughtful expression on his lean, handsome face.

"I have no objection, gentlemen," he said then, "to your wanting a larger return for your labors. But I don't like Red Leech coming in here with his so-called army. I don't like that part of your plans at all."

"Do you know him, John?" Bronsen asked.

"I know his reputation as a terrorist and bully. I've heard of his insatiable lust for women. Keeps a veritable harem up at that fort of his, so I'm told."

"Yes, we've heard all that, too," Owens said. "But he also has a reputation for licking Mexican armies at their own damned game."

"And without him," Bronsen said, "we couldn't attempt to put our goods across the river. Unless, of course, you'd recruit an army of your own."

Lime put his hand up, shook his head. "That would be out of the question. From an operation such as you gentlemen are planning there are bound to be repercussions. Loud enough to be heard clear to Washington." He flicked the ash from his panatella, smiled at them. "And as you probably all know," he added urbanely, "I may have other fish to fry in that direction."

There was polite laughter. Bronsen and Owens had heard that their youngish sheriff was ambitious to test his influence outside of Brownsville, that he was preparing to challenge formidable old Sam Houston for his seat in the U.S. Senate and control of state politics.

"Those fish, John," Bronsen said, "can get expensive. Votes cost money."

"All contributions," Lime said, "are gratefully accepted."

"The Merchants Association would be proud to have our own sheriff sitting for us in the Senate," Bronsen said. "And we'd be happy to contribute to his campaign — out of any extra profits we might make in the near future."

Lime blew a cloud of smoke toward the ceiling. "Instead of Red Leech," he asked, "couldn't you bribe the Mexican general?"

"We've tried that," Ezra Owens said, "and gotten badly stung. They're just not to be trusted."

"We need Leech and his gunfighters," Bronsen said flatly.

The sheriff looked at him. "All right," he said. "But on three conditions. Number one, that Leech and his men be quartered beyond the city limits. Number two, that you begin your operation within one week after

Leech arrives in this territory. And number three, that Leech and company do not return here when their work is concluded." He smiled. "And to guarantee that I want a bond in the sum of five thousand dollars posted for each condition."

The merchants looked from the smiling man to each other, nodded. Owens got to his feet.

"We'll post the bonds in the morning, Sheriff," he said.

"Good. Of course, they're forfeit in any event."

"I assumed as much," Bronsen said. "Our contribution to your campaign."

"Your first one, gentlemen," Lime said cheerfully. "I'm told that General Houston has almost unlimited resources at his command."

The businessmen left the meeting. The embargo was put in effect next day and the booming trade between the United States and Mexico — via Brownsville and Matamoros — ground to a shattering halt. For sixty days not a shipment crossed the river, not one of any importance, and the eager Mexican buyers who came over to see what had happened were advised to quadruple their orders for cotton and tools and await delivery some dark night in the near future. The Mexicans paid their money and went back home to wait and worry. The goods they'd bought, meanwhile, piled up on the Brownsville docks, filled warehouses to the bursting point.

Red Leech, escorted by Lash Wall and seven unshaven, rifle-bearing bodyguards, rode into Brownsville when the embargo was in its forty-fifth day. And on that same afternoon six spruced-up mules were taking Rig Bogan and his red wagon south out of San Antonio.

Bert Bronsen, Ezra Owens and Ed Boone were a committee of three who took the renegade and his lieutenant to a rendezvous with John Lime. Leech, mellowed by the quart of whisky he had consumed since breakfast, took the slender man's hand and gazed down at him with a benevolent leer.

"So you got this town in your back pocket, do yuh?" he boomed.

Lime withdrew his hand, hooded his eyes. "I enforce the law here, yes," he answered.

"So I hear, brother! And, brother, you know what you did one year ago?" He turned to Lash Wall. "Ain't this the one?" he asked.

Wall, his cool gaze on Lime's face, nodded briefly.

"You know what you did?" Leech repeated.

"What?"

"Why, you sonofabitch, you hung one of my boys!" Leech roared and it was hard to tell whether he was happy about it or enraged. "Stretched poor old Chug Murrow, that's what you did!"

"Murrow?" Lime repeated. "I think he's the one who held up the Diamond Bar and shot Saul Petit."

"Wouldn't be surprised!" Leech agreed. "But, brother, you went and *hung* old Chug. One of my boys!"

Lime waited patiently until the echoes died away. Then he said, "And I'd do it again, Leech. To any of your gang."

"Me included?" Leech demanded, grinning through his beard.

"You and any man who breaks the law in Brownsville," Lime told him calmly.

Leech thumped him on the back. "Don't bite off what you can't chew, brother," he shouted at him with a great pealing laugh. "And, brother, I'm some mouthful!"

Lime measured the red-haired giant for a moment, glanced at Bert Bronsen. "Have you explained the conditions yet?"

"We, ah, haven't had a chance."

"What conditions, Sheriff?" Lash Wall asked quietly.

"Yeah, what conditions?" Red Leech demanded.

Lime ignored them, gazed steadily at

111

Bronsen. The merchant cleared his throat nervously.

"We have agreed to certain things," Bronsen began. "The first is that you and your men are to stay out of the city. We have a very nice house prepared for you outside town. It's large and comfortable and will make a fine headquarters."

"But we're not good enough to come into your town, is that it, Sheriff?" Lash Wall asked. He smiled then. "Or maybe we're a little *too* good for you to handle?"

Leech roared an approving laugh. "You tell 'im, Lash! You tell 'im!"

John Lime and Lash Wall locked glances. There was mutual respect.

"Explain condition number two," Lime said to Bronsen.

"We're to begin the operation in one week," Bronsen said. "Will your men all be here by then?"

"My boys are to hell and gone, brother! How do I know when they'll get here?"

"And there's another thing, Sheriff," Lash Wall said. "I want to go over the route foot by foot. Especially where we cross the Rio with these goods. That'll take time."

"How much time?"

"More than a week. Two weeks. Maybe three."

"Two," Lime told him and somehow they

had bypassed Red Leech. Lash Wall nodded.

"Two weeks it is," he said. "Any more conditions?"

"You and your gang are to leave this territory when your work for the merchants is concluded," Lime said.

"Suppose we like it here, brother?" Red Leech demanded. "Who's gonna chase us out?"

"Soldier," Lime said, sounding very much like a former army captain, "soldier, you've made your rep against Mexicans. If you've a mind to try your bandit tactics against some Texans I'm sure you'll be accommodated."

"You threatenin' Red Leech, brother?" the giant thundered. Lash Wall stepped between them.

"We're down here on business, Sheriff," he said peaceably. "After we're done maybe we'll consider your invitation." He smiled. "Any other conditions?"

"No, mister, that's all."

Wall turned to Leech. "Let's go see our headquarters, Big Red," he suggested. "Get ourselves set up."

"Damn right! You know somethin', Lash? I ain't had my siesta! Been ridin' since mornin'!" Then he thought of something else. "And by Judas, Lash, I ain't had a woman for a week!"

"We'll take care of you, Big Red," Lash Wall told him, turning the man around and easing him toward the door of Lime's office. He looked back. "Nice meeting you, Sheriff," he said.

"Been my pleasure, mister," Lime answered cordially.

The house that the merchants had provided for Red Leech's headquarters was just as Bert Bronsen had described it — a large, comfortable hacienda that had once been the property of a wealthy Mexican. Visiting Spanish royalty had slept beneath its roof, and General Santa Ana, and just about every very important personage passing through the region. It was a house rich in history and full of memories — but none so rich and gaudy as the ones Red Leech and company gave it within twenty-four hours of moving in.

It became the house that never slept. True, there were saloons in the city that stayed open around-the-clock but no place in Brownsville maintained the driving, riotous pace of drinking, brawling and carousing of Leech's "army." The capable Lash Wall had sent for a total of thirty of them, and each hour, each day, each night, another one or two or three of the far-flung gang would arrive. Old acquaintances were renewed boisterously, there was a fresh excuse for a party, and the ball kept rolling and rolling of its own wild momentum.

To one Turkey Forbes was delegated the role of official greeter and host. As host, Turkey's main responsibility was to keep the wine, women and song in ample supply, and all day and all night two trains passed each other on the road to Brownsville. The wagons and carriages going to the city contained empty whisky kegs and exhausted, sleeping girls whose garter belts bulged with money. The train going to the hacienda outside of town carried full kegs and a fresh load of gay, bright-eyed, companionable young females who were ready and eager for anything. The piano player and the fiddler stayed at the house, making music even with their eyes closed and growing richer beyond all expectations.

On the third evening of the *Gran Fiesta* a party of three dust-begrimed, hard-faced riders rode into the courtyard and were greeted enthusiastically by Lash Wall.

"Fred Perrott! Jules!" he shouted warmly. "Sam Gill! Sure glad you three fighters made it!"

The trio of gunmen took the homage as if it were their due, murmured a greeting in return and dismounted.

"How were pickings up Uvalde way?" Wall asked.

"So-so," Fred Perrott grunted. There could

be no mistaking him and Jules for brothers. Both were tall and rawboned, with big, rough-looking hands and hard-muscled bodies. Their faces were even more alike — thin, hawkish noses, high cheekbones, thin lips and dark eyes set deep in their faces beneath protruding foreheads. Their hair was long and unkempt, the color of dried hay. Sam Gill was shorter and thicker through the chest. His face was square, his eyes wide-spaced, and there was an expression of truculent obstinacy about him even when he felt relaxed. It was a toss up between the three as to who owned the quickest gun or the most will to use it.

"So-so," Fred Perrott repeated. "Picked up a little on the way down, though."

"That so?"

"Got us a stage outside of Hondo," Fred Perrott said conversationally. "Almost lost our stake in some little burg called — what was the name of that town, Jules?"

"Aura," Jules Perrott said. "Gah-damn muleskinner, winnin' and grinnin'. Tried to rub our noses in it."

"He's done winnin'," Sam Gill said slyly. "And grinnin'."

"Well, come in, boys, and say hello to Big Red."

"Yeah. What the hell's all the racket inside?"

"Somebody's throwing a party," Lash Wall

116

told them. "In honor of the biggest job we ever got next to."

"Lead me to it," Fred Perrott said. "I'm in the mood for some cuttin' loose."

As soon as they entered the hacienda they were greeted with a wild and drunken roar of welcome. Girls squealed and the fiddle jumped to new life.

"Pull the plug on another keg!" Red Leech shouted overall. "Three stray lambs has joined the flock!"

Somebody fired a gun into the high ceiling. Somebody else fell out a window. A girl squealed on the top floor. The party started all over again.

Things had begun to taper off, but not much, by the time the last two of the summoned gunfighters arrived at headquarters.

"What in hell happened to you, Wynt?" Red Leech demanded. Wynt Jenkins, carrying his arm in a sling to favor the bullet-grazed collarbone, scowled fiercely.

"Some dirty jasper up the line got the drop on me," he growled. "Leastways, I'm better off than old Prado."

"Prado?" Lash Wall asked. "What happened to him?"

"Cashed in his stack," Sherm Moore answered. "Stepped on a tiger's tail sure enough."

"Sam Prado dead," Red Leech said, subdued for once. "Never thought I'd hear bad news like that."

"Let me get this straight," Lash Wall interrupted. "The same fella took you and Prado both?"

Wynt nodded.

"And where were you?" Wall asked Sherm Moore.

"Standin' there with my left foot in hell," Sherm answered. "And I ain't ashamed to be still alive to tell about it. I mean, Lash, this boy was primed."

"We'll sure miss Prado's gun," Red Leech said mournfully.

"Yeah, Big Red, we sure will," Lash said, his voice thoughtful. "But I wouldn't mind having the gun that got him."

"Well, we ain't and what the hell?" Leech said. "How many are we now, anyhow?"

"Sherm and Wynt make thirty-five," Wall answered, "but I don't know if Wynt can handle himself in a fight."

"He'll be able to do somethin'," Leech assured him. "You been over the trail like you said you would?"

Wall nodded. "Going to draw a map tonight."

"How does it look?"

The lieutenant shrugged. "Bronsen and Owens want us to make the crossing just south of Davis Landing," he said. "I admit it's narrower there, but if I had my druthers

I'd get across the river farther north. Up around Roma."

"You tell 'em that?"

"I mentioned it. They said they were risking over a million dollars in goods and they'd pick the crossing place."

Leech's little eyes lit up. "Over a million, eh? And we get a tenth?"

"Unless we did it the other way around," Lash Wall said, smiling.

"Other way around?"

"Or threatened to at the last minute, Big Red. Get Mr. Bronsen and his friends to sweeten our end of the pot another tenth or so."

Red Leech grinned wickedly. "Boy, I don't know where you get these ideas, but they sure are beauties! And that reminds me, where the hell's that big blonde-headed girl today? I like her good enough to keep permanent."

"She'll be back tonight, Big Red," Turkey Forbes promised.

"She better. And where's Jules Perrott lately? I ain't seen him around lately."

"Jules' been slippin' into town last couple of nights," brother Fred answered. "He don't like it when he's told he can't go to a place."

"What can he do there that he can't do right here?" Leech asked.

"Aw, you know Jules," Fred Perrott said.

"He's just got an ornery streak. Bad as our pa."

"Well, I hope he don't get ornery with that sheriff," Lash Wall said then. Big Red scowled at him darkly.

"You afraid of that little badge toter, by God?"

"You know better, Big Red. But we don't have Prado and we only got a part of Wynt. We lose any more boys and this convoy operation could get to be a real chore."

"Why? What've the Mex got over there?"

"Troops," Wall answered laconically. "Took Dirge Pine over for a little reconnoiter night before last. There's an army waiting for us there, Big Red. A thousand of 'em. And guns aplenty."

"Well, hell! We licked the bastards afore, didn't we?"

"Fighting our style," Lash Wall reminded the leader. "Hit and run. This time we got to take a million in bulky goods across that Rio. And when we're hit we got to stay and fight."

"Lash, gah-damn it, you're gonna spoil my fun! Where's that big blonde-headed baby o'mine?"

SEVEN

"W E COULD MAKE it to Brownsville tonight,"
Buchanan told the girl. The sun was
a red ball in the west and their horses had
drunk their fill of the stream water.

"Whatever you say," Cristy replied. Her
pretty face was filmed with dust, weary-
looking. Her hair was awry. But she sat her
saddle as straight as she was able. Even
more.

"Tired?"

"No," she lied.

"On the other hand —"

"What?"

"Just thinking out loud, ma'am. Three,
four more hours in the saddle and all I'll
be looking for in Brownsville is a bed."

"Instead of the men who killed Bogan?"
she asked quietly.

"Yeh. So there doesn't seem much point
in pushing these horses today."

"No," she agreed. "Let's be kind to the
horses."

Buchanan looked at her. "Meaning you
are a little wore out?"

Cristy sighed, nodded. "Riding a trail is a

man's game," she confessed.

"Why didn't you say something?" He dismounted, came to assist her down.

"You haven't been exactly approachable," she said. "Your thoughts are on other things." She leaned down into his waiting arms, felt herself floated to the ground effortlessly. Buchanan stepped back, his manner impersonal.

"There's plenty of squirrels around here," he said. "You duck your face in that stream and I'll see about supper."

"Squirrels?"

"Squirrel pie," Buchanan said. "The mountain man's chicken."

"You eat squirrels?"

"Well, I'd never order one in a restaurant."

"I *couldn't*," the girl said squeamishly. "I can't even think about it."

"Well," Buchanan said, "I could go upstream a ways. Might be some beavers around."

"Stop!" she cried. "Please stop!" Then she thought of something, turned to her saddlebag. "Oh, thank the Lord!" she murmured. "I just remembered that I brought some food. Bacon and beans. Is that all right?"

"Sounds fine."

"Squirrel!" she said, taking the things from the saddlebag. "Beaver!"

"They got better manners than the pig

that bacon was sliced off of," Buchanan pointed out. "Howsomever —"

"Howsomever, it's civilized," she said.

Buchanan chuckled lightly. "You'd be surprised, ma'am, who started making squirrel pie."

"Who?"

"Some high quality folks in the Virginia Colony. Taste for it spread to South Carolina."

"You're making that up!"

Buchanan took an oath with his upraised hand. "South Carolina's famous for squirrel pie. You mean you never saw one of those great big juicy fox squinels when you was up there?"

"Buchanan, you're a big tease. Have you ever been in Carolina?"

He smiled, shook his head. "I will, though, by-an'-by. Going to see it all before I'm through."

"Is that your ambition — to travel?"

"*Ambition?* No, it's my perdition. My ambition, at the moment, is to get a fire going under this hog's hide and pea beans. And while it's cookin' to soak my own hide in that runnin' water."

He lit a fire, improvised a wetwood grill, bid the girl a temporary adieu and tramped upstream for his privacy. Fifteen minutes later he signalled his return and stepped into the clearing. It was dusk now, and the firelight was warm and cheerful.

"That water was cold, wasn't it?" he said, noticing that her hair and skin still glistened with moisture.

"Yes," Cristy said, her voice low. She sat close to the fire.

"Did you peel all the way down?" He stirred the beans.

"Yes."

"Did you feel that counter-current? Where you sit?"

"Yes."

Buchanan turned the sizzling bacon over.

"Buchanan."

He glanced at her. "What?"

"I — I have a confession to make. I did something — something terrible. I followed you. I watched — like Joseph in the Bible —"

Buchanan's laughter was a thing to hear. "I wish I'd've known about *that*," he said. "I'd've strutted like a peacock!"

"But I'm so ashamed of myself," the girl protested. "I don't know what came over me to do such a thing!"

"If I'd only known," Buchanan repeated happily. He served her beans and bacon.

"You don't think I did wrong — to spy on you?"

"I didn't feel a thing," Buchanan assured her. "Say, this is good bacon. Good as the steak that Chinaman cooked for me last night."

The girl studied his profile in the flickering firelight. "Chang was impressed with you, too," she said. "Before I left this morning he told me you were going to be a very important man. That you were going to have the biggest ranch in Texas."

"Yeh, he told me, too."

"Isn't that what you want — a ranch of your own?"

"I don't know," Buchanan said, staring into the blaze. "I don't know what I want for my own."

"A woman?" she asked and he swung his head to her.

"Not for my own, no," he said. "Not yet." He looked back into the fire. "Not yet, and especially not now."

"Because of this thing that's eating at you, this need for vengeance?" she said with a trace of anger. "Is that the only thing that's important to you now?"

Buchanan kept silent.

"There were three of them!" she suddenly cried at him. "Three of them against one of you! Do you think you're infallible? Don't you know that everybody runs out of luck sometime?"

"Hey, take it easy," Buchanan said.

"I'm sorry," Cristy said, getting control of her voice. "I'll — I'll try not to speak my thoughts like a silly woman."

"You haven't said anything silly."

She was quiet for a long moment, marshaling her thoughts. "Buchanan," she said. "Tom. I've sat at a table with men for nearly a year, dealing them cards, and all the odds of blackjack are with the dealer. But I've had them come in — like your friend Bogan the other night — and nothing can go wrong for them. You say you'll pay sixteen and they have sixteen. You say you'll pay twenty-one and they turn up the black jack. Have you seen them?"

"Sure."

"They even do everything against all the rules. They go for five and under with a seven-six showing. And they win."

"I never did."

"And they win," the girl said again. "Then you can see a change in them. They think the gambler's prayer has been finally answered, that they can ride their luck forever and do no wrong." She took a deep breath. "You were lucky last night with those gunmen," Cristy said. "I thought about it afterward. If he had fired that shotgun you would have been killed. If you'd been standing with your back to the doors when the other one shot at you —"

"He didn't and I wasn't," Buchanan said.

"But it was pure chance that neither thing happened!" she insisted. "And now you're going to press your luck against three more of them! It won't hold out, Tom!"

He let a few calming seconds go by before he spoke.

"Don't get blackjack mixed up with life," Buchanan said with a different quality to his voice. "You move around enough and you eventually run across all the types. Like that fella with the shotgun — the big mouth. Him, he can't kill you without making you squirm some." Buchanan turned to her. "Plugging him first wasn't lucky, ma'am," he said, "that was prudent. The same for not standing there with my back to the doors. That was a plain case of caution."

"Do you mean to say you thought you'd be shot at?"

Buchanan smiled. "I mean to say I make a sizable target," he told her. "And as for pressing my luck against those three bushwhackers," he added, "I'm one up on them already."

"How?"

"They don't know I'm coming," Buchanan said.

Cristy had no ready answer to that logic and a pensive silence fell between them. Buchanan rose from the fire, got their blankets and set them the same distance apart as if he were traveling with another man.

"Early start tomorrow. Let's turn in," he

said and the girl knew that the time of easy relaxation was over for him. His mind was back on the mission that was taking him to the border.

"I'm going to sit here for a while," Cristy said. "I couldn't possibly get to sleep this early."

"Suit yourself," Buchanan said, sliding beneath his blanket. "Tomorrow night you can get back to your regular routine."

"What do you mean, my regular routine?" she said sharply.

Buchanan raised his head, surprised. "No offense," he explained. "I just meant you could do as you pleased. Stay up all night and sleep all morning."

"Is that the kind of life you think I want?" she demanded.

"Sounds pretty good to me," Buchanan said, lowering his head again. "Well, good night —"

The girl got to her feet, came to stand above him.

"I don't want to stay up all night and sleep all morning," she said, her voice intense. "I want to live like other women. With a man."

"You will," Buchanan said drowsily, getting comfortable on his side. "You'll get whatever you want."

"How do you know I will?"

"Because you're a real fine girl. 'Night."

Cristy stood looking down at him for a long moment before turning away. She knew that she couldn't have made it any plainer to him than she had. Nor could he.

They arrived in teeming, rowdy-looking Brownsville before noon the next day. Arrived after nearly four hours' riding with hardly a complete sentence spoken between them. Buchanan, not suspecting that he had wounded the girl's pride the night before, got his first hint of her attitude when she declined to be helped down from her horse. And his second when she held out her hand to him, man-fashion.

"Thank you for the safe journey on the trail," she said and the man thought there was something wryly mocking in the way she emphasized the word "safe."

"You're welcome," he said.

"And good luck in your manhunting."

"Thanks," he said, looking around. "This could be a likely town to start with." When he looked back she was walking away from him, full of confidence, self-reliance, and even in the tight-fitting pants and shirt he was reminded again of San Francisco. "So long," he called after her, but she didn't turn.

Buchanan shrugged, then frowned. The girl's steps had carried opposite a saloon entrance just as two hardcase types emerged drunkenly into the sunlight. Cristy moved around them lithely, kept going. So did the liquored pair, in the same direction and in obvious pursuit. And Buchanan made four.

Cristy, full of her own stinging thoughts, was unaware of being followed. Unaware, too, of the dark alley looming on her left. An instant later rough hands were clamped on her arms and she was being forced relentlessly into the alleyway.

Buchanan moved, swiftly — but across his path and into the alleyway before him darted a slim man dressed all in black. The man felled one of Cristy's would-be attackers with a flat-handed blow at the base of the neck. The second one obligingly swung around and was struck twice in the solar plexus and on the point of his jaw. He went down soundlessly.

Buchanan stood there, watching in admiration an expert at work. There wasn't anything else he could do but watch.

"Are you injured, Miss?"

Cristy blinked her eyes at him — he was hardly taller than herself — and shook her head bewilderedly. The man turned, gave Buchanan a brief, appraising glance, and stepped into the street. He put his fingers to his lips and whistled shrilly, went back into the alley.

Now he raised his black hat to Cristy and

bowed his head. "John Lime, Miss, Sheriff of Brownsville," he said in a courtly voice. "And my deepest apologies for what happened here."

"Nothing happened, really," the girl said. "But thank you very much —"

There was a commotion then as three deputies entered the alleyway from three different directions, picked up the dazed pair from the ground and carted them off without a word.

"Did I detect a Southern accent, Miss?" John Lime said urbanely, offering Christy his arm and escorting her past the useless-feeling Buchanan.

"I'm from South Carolina," Cristy said.

"Well! My original home is Virginia."

"Well! What a small world we live in." She smiled at him. "My name, Mr. Lime, is Cristina Ford, and you must excuse my strange costume."

"Miss Ford, a lady is a lady no matter what her garb."

"Well, thank you, sir." She glanced over her shoulder. "And may I introduce Mr. Buchanan?"

Lime gave Buchanan a longer appraisal, offered his hand. They shook.

"Are you, ah, *with* Miss Ford, sir?"

"I don't think so," Buchanan said.

"Mr. Buchanan provided me his protection on the journey from Aura," Cristy said

131

and Buchanan noted how really Southern her voice had suddenly become.

"And you took over from there," Buchanan said. "Some nice job, too."

John Lime didn't acknowledge the praise. He still had questions for the tall man with the well-worn Colt on his hip.

"You're in Brownsville on business, Buchanan?"

"Maybe."

"Maybe?"

"I'm not sure yet."

The answer didn't please the lawman. "Are you connected with Red Leech?"

"No," Buchanan answered, thinking that the name rang a bell. Who had mentioned Red Leech?

"What is your line of work?" Lime pressed.

"Well, I was in the freight business for about a week," Buchanan answered truthfully. "I came down here to sort of clear up a few odds and ends."

Lime's unyielding gaze went to the Colt.

"But you are not with the Leech gang?"

"Didn't even know he had one."

"Well, he does. And this town is off-limits to every member of it. This town is also against lawlessness, no matter what you may have heard elsewhere."

"I did hear it was lively," Buchanan said.

"Lively and prosperous and growing," Lime told him. "A place of recreation and commerce, the queen city of the Rio. But law-abiding."

"That's fine with me, Sheriff."

Lime was finished with him and turned back to Cristy.

"Miss Ford," he said gallantly, "I wonder if I might have the honor of showing you our city?"

"I'd be delighted, Mr. Lime," Cristy said.

"And perhaps you'd dine with me at the Palace Hotel?"

"Thank you very much, but I really couldn't. Not in this costume."

"Then let's correct that situation immediately," John Lime said, offering his arm again. "At Madame Maude's I'm sure you'll find the latest fashions."

"Oh, I couldn't. Really —"

"But I insist. After all, we Southerners must set the example in hospitality." He nodded to Buchanan. "Good day, sir," he said and swept Cristy away.

Buchanan, suddenly all alone in the alley, moved out onto the boardwalk, stood there with his hands on his hips and watched the departing couple. Now there, he thought, goes one fast-moving gent, and didn't miss noticing how passersby opened up a passage for the sheriff of Brownsville, stood aside and relinquished the right of way without question. Some punkins, Mr. Lime, he thought and then smiled inwardly at himself. Man, alive, don't get sore at him for charming Cristy right out of her boots. She's the marryin' kind, like you told yourself last night.

Buchanan went off in the opposite direction in search of a meal.

EIGHT

LASH WALL STOOD in the courtyard of the hacienda and watched the last wagon train of party girls and empty kegs depart for Brownsville. Bronsen and Owens had ridden out to the palace of fun earlier in the day and been indelibly shocked at the full-blown orgy they found in full swing. They'd come to inform Red Leech that the merchants were ready to end their embargo and begin the great smuggling operation.

"Hell, me and the boys are ready, brother!" Leech bawled at them fuzzily and would have fallen on his beard had not his bosomy blonde friend pulled him back down on the couch. Wall had taken charge then, ushering the worried businessmen back to their carriage and assuring them that Leech's army would be in the saddle within forty-eight hours. Bronsen and Owens looked very doubtful as they rode out.

If you're unhappy now, Lash thought, wait until you hear about that extra ten per cent you're giving us.

His next task that morning was to roam the three floors of the house and herd the

135

women into the wagons and buggies. He saved Big Red until last, happily found him passed out, and bribed the blonde with an additional ten-dollar coin to depart with her sisters. In the late afternoon, when Leech woke up roaring for food, drink and companionship in that order, Wall sat down for a council of war.

"We got to sober up and go to work, Big Red," he told the scowling leader. "We start pushing their cotton tomorrow night. And we'll be pushing it every night for the next two weeks."

"You mean to say I can't fight Mexicans drunk or sober?" Leech snarled belligerently.

"You can, Big Red," Wall said diplomatically. "But the rest of the boys are only human. And you've got to set them an example."

"Yeah?"

"Sure. That's why you're running things around here."

"I don't seem to be running this shebang, by God!"

"You will when we mount up," Wall told him. "All I've been doing is the staff work, handling the little details. Tomorrow night it's up to you whether we do it or we don't."

"I guess you're right, Lash. Like usual." He lumbered to his feet, tossed the lamb bone he'd been shredding into a corner.

"Put the crew on rations starting now. A quart a day per man."

"How about half a quart?"

"Jesus! All right, all right! And no more chummin'. We're a bunch of monks till the job's done. And Jules Perrott and everybody else sticks close to headquarters. Anything else you can think of?"

"The boys could check their guns and ammo, Big Red. And look the animals over from head to foot."

"Yeah. Go pass the word. Tell 'em I said so and I'll break any bastard in two who gives any argument."

Lash Wall passed the word and it was accepted at face value by all but Jules Perrott.

"My guns are always in good shape," he said surlily. "And so's my horse."

"Meaning you're planning another trip into town?"

"Meaning I don't like to be ordered around. I can make my own rules."

"Jules, what's the big attraction in Brownsville? You got a girl there?"

"I got me a tinhorn gambler on the hook and I don't aim to let him off."

"How much you ahead?"

"Six hundred. Tonight I'm going to bet the roll and break the little son."

"Suppose it's the other way round?"

"It won't be."

"But suppose it is."

Perrott shrugged his bony shoulders. "So I lose," he said.

Lash Wall shook his head. "I've played cards with you, Jules," he said. "You don't like to lose."

"Whatta you mean?"

"I mean you brood about it. You climb inside of a bottle. And then you get mean and start to make trouble."

"Listen, Wall —"

"You listen. You make trouble in Brownsville and that sheriff'll be on you like a blanket. Stay here tonight, Jules. We need your gun for the job. Understand?"

Perrott's thin lips formed a smile. "Sure, Lash," he said. "I understand."

"Those are Leech's orders, Jules. Personal."

"Sure. Big Red himself. I understand."

One hour after the sun set Jules Perrott rode out of the hacienda toward the beckoning lights of Brownsville. Turkey Forbes reported it to Lash Wall and Wall passed a hand across his cheek, finished the gesture with fingers crossed. Somehow he couldn't shake the premonition that this was Jules' night to lose.

Buchanan visited Brownsville's five hotels — if that was the word for them — without finding anyone named Perrott or Gill registered. Playing a long shot, to be sure, but in this case justified by the simple fact that he had no clear picture of the three men he was looking for. To say that they were tough and swaggering and liked to play cards hardly distinguished them in this man's town.

He wasn't discouraged, though — it wasn't his nature to be — and when he learned in the fifth hotel that a night's lodging cost twenty-five cents he decided to invest that much of the two dollars he still owned and continue the search in Brownsville for at least another twenty-four hours.

"We got a fifty-cent accommodation, too," the clerk said, bouncing Buchanan's silver coin on the desk to test its ring.

"What's wrong with the twenty-five-cent one?"

"Nothin', mister. We also got a dollar room. That includes a girl and a towel."

"Sounds like a real bargain," Buchanan agreed. "But just slip me my six-bits change and I'll scout up my own entertainment."

"Suit yourself, mister," the clerk said. "Take those stairs two flights up, and then take your chances."

Buchanan climbed to the third floor and found himself in a crowded, noisy, highly fragrant dormitory. The four walls were lined with double bunks, some fifty of them, and five more-or-less even rows of iron cots filled the center area of the barracks-type room. Men's voices filled the air, men milled to and fro, played cards, drank whisky, read newspapers, slept soundly, just sat on the edge of their cots and stared into space.

Buchanan worked his way toward a far corner, asked if a particular lower bunk was taken when he got there, tossed his hat on it when told it wasn't. He unhitched his gunrig then, emptied the cylinder of the Colt and sat down with it to do a little cleaning and adjusting. A fine piece of hardware, he thought, and was proud of it. But up in Aura, night before last, he'd detected a slight sluggishness in the mechanism. A man gets used to a hair-trigger and he's just plain spoiled by anything less.

He worked on the trigger with the small blade in his jackknife, tightening the delicate mainspring infinitesimally, testing the action studiously, and as he worked, listened to the jabberwocky all around him.

Chaz Murto, Buchanan learned, had lost three teeth in a brawl at the Lone Star Saloon.

Jack Boyd, on the other hand, had cleaned up at Faro's place.

And did everybody hear that the fiesta out to the hacienda had finally ended?

No!

Yes! They brought a load of girls back as

usual this morning but none went out again.

What the hell was Leech's Army doing down here, anyhow? somebody asked and Buchanan's head came up at mention of the name again.

Leech, a man answered knowingly, was fixing to take over the whole border country. Set up the Republic of the Rio Grande, with him as major domo.

He'll have to get past John Lime first.

Looks like a filly did the job already.

Say, did you see them together? Lime paraded her around town like he had the Queen of Sheba on his arm. Never saw the man smile before.

And some looker, too. First girl I ever saw him take a shine to in public.

"Excuse me," someone said close to Buchanan's ear and he turned to find a dapperly dressed man seated beside him on the bunk. The man stared at the Colt as if fascinated.

"Howdy."

"You sure like that gun, don't you?"

"An old friend of mine," Buchanan said.

"Never saw such loving care before. Use it much?"

"Now and then."

"Pretty good with it, though?"

"Fair," Buchanan conceded. "Got a tendency to hit left of center."

"How much left?"

"A good sixteenth of an inch." He held up his thumb and forefinger, separated them the width of a .45 slug. "Missed that far night before last," he reported.

"But you got him?"

"Yeh."

The little man stood up, extended his hand eagerly. "I'm Hal Harper," he said. "Own a blackjack table over at the Crystal Palace."

Buchanan shook his hand, looked on him with interest.

"My name's Buchanan," he said. "You deal blackjack?"

"Honest Hal and an honest game," the gambler said.

"I believe it. You got any customers name of Perrott? Two brothers? Fella name of Sam Gill?"

Hal Harper shook his head. "Friends of yours?"

Buchanan smiled. "Not exactly, no."

"They owe you some money?"

"Something like that." He flipped the cylinder open, satisfied at last with the trigger, and began dropping in the lead. Harper watched with great interest.

"I don't place those names," he said. "Wish I could help you."

"Thanks."

"But you could help me, friend. About

twenty-five dollars worth."

Buchanan looked up from his loading. From time to time today he'd given a random thought to his sorry finances, reduced at the moment to one lonely dollar.

"What would I do for the twenty-five?" he asked.

"Keep an eye on me tonight. And that big gun handy."

"Why?

"It's like this," the gambler said confidentally. "I've had a hardcase on my hands all week. A gunny with the blood in his eye, if you know what I mean."

"On the prod," Buchanan said.

"Right. And he's picked my game, personal, out of all the blackjack dealt in this town. Every night he's there, waiting for me."

"You beating him?"

Harper shook his small head. "No, and that's the point. He's, I guess, five, six hundred into me. But some night, maybe tonight, things are bound to go my way. And, friend, I'm scared. So scared of what this jasper will do that I'd just about decided not to go to work tonight. Then," he said, "I got to watching you work that shooter and decided to make you this proposition. How about it, Buchanan?"

Buchanan's eyes held the gambler's fast.

"Proddy or not," he said, "this fella gets an honest deal?"

"Never cheated another man in my life," Harper said and Buchanan believed him.

"Then I'd be glad to watch your game," he said, smiling. "And grateful for the twenty-five."

"Well, fine! Say, I'm hungry. How about you?"

"I would be," Buchanan admitted, "if I had an advance on my night's wage."

The gambler's hand darted beneath his coat, came back holding a thick roll of bills. He deftly peeled off two tens and a five, handed them to his new bodyguard.

"And the meal's on me," Harper added. "I got an idea my luck is riding high."

They left their lodgings, and enroute to the restaurant Hal Harper gave a rapid-fire account of his life and times. He'd been born in New York City, the first of nine children whose father had migrated from Ireland and joined the police force.

"The old man's an Inspector now, but, of course, he disowned me a long time ago."

Harper had left the crowded home in New York when he was fifteen, taken a job on the boat that plied the Hudson River to Albany.

"Supposed to be working for the line," he said, "but what I really did was mark for the gamblers. Mark the passengers who had the best luggage and tipped big."

He did that for a year, and when one of the gamblers invited him to come along down to New Orleans for the winter he accepted.

"Is that town all they say?" Buchanan asked.

"Ain't nobody said it all about New Orleans," Harper said, his voice wistful.

"How come you left?"

"A woman," Harper said. "A Creole gal with a Creole husband. I wasn't going to be much good to her dead."

He had declined the invitation to duel the husband, an expert swordsman, and left New Orleans for the West, via Missouri and Kansas.

"Ever get to San Francisco?" Buchanan asked.

"Ever get there? Friend, I spent the five happiest years of my life on the Barbary Coast. You can have Paris and London," Harper said, "if you'll give me that Frisco town!"

"How come you left?"

"A woman," Harper said. "Sweetest little gal I ever laid eyes on. Always smiling and good-natured."

"She had a husband?"

"Me," the gambler said sadly. "I married her. Never saw a person change overnight once they had a wedding ring. Wanted me to give up gambling. Wanted me to give up whisky. Started coming down to my game nights and raising three kinds of hell."

A cantankerous wife had chased him clear out of California, made him miss the big gold strike and the chance of a lifetime to make his fortune. He'd tried his luck in Mexico for a time, then slowly drifted eastward along the Rio.

"Now I'm in Brownsville," he said as they took their seats in the restaurant. "Going to build my stake to ten thousand and take another go at New Orleans."

"That's my destination, too," Buchanan said. "Sometime soon, I hope."

"Really?"

"Got a friend there with a good deal. Fella named Duke Hazeltine —"

"Duke? You know the duke?"

"We've split a bottle or two. Met him over in El Paso."

"Well, Duke Hazeltine is one of the best! A real gent."

"Glad to hear you say so," Buchanan said, studying the menu the pretty little waitress had brought. "What's good?" he asked her.

"The steak."

"Is it long or thick?"

"Thick," she said.

"That's it, then. A little underdone on the inside, please."

"Same here, Tillie," Harper said, then had

his attention caught by something across the room. "Well, say, she *is* a looker!" he said enthusiastically.

"Who?"

"The blonde that just arrived with the man himself. Been hearing about her all afternoon."

Buchanan turned his head to catch the grand entrance of Miss Cristina Ford and Sheriff Lime. His trail partner had shed the boots and levis for a gown of gleaming blue silk, with a bustle in the back, and her golden-hued hair was piled atop her head in a maze of ringlets. She looked to Buchanan like one of those elegant paintings that hung in the posh bars of San Francisco.

"How'd you like to spend an evening with that?" Hal Harper asked, his voice hushed.

Buchanan turned his head back around, smiled to himself. "Be something to remember," he said.

"Haughty as a queen, though," Harper said. "Cold. Wouldn't you say so?"

"Never can tell," Buchanan said. "The way they look and the way they feel can be two different things."

The dapper little gambler laughed. "Well, boy, you and me aren't likely to find out how she feels. She's way beyond our reach."

"Miles and miles," Buchanan said.

Their steaks arrived soon afterward, and though Buchanan gave his usual undivided attention to the meal, Hal Harper spent most of his time stealing glances across the room. Suddenly his eyes dropped to his plate and he stiffened.

"You all right, Harper?"

"I think I'm in bad trouble," the gambler murmured shakily. "John Lime is headed for this table."

"Trouble about what?"

"For staring at his woman. This is a hanging town and he runs it —"

Buchanan put his fork down, swung his head around out of curiosity. The sheriff, sure enough, was making right for them. Then he was there.

"Evening, Buchanan."

"Hi, Sheriff. You know Hal Harper?"

"I know his reputation," Lime said and Harper winced. "He deals an honest game. Miss Ford would like you and your companion to join us in a brandy."

"Us?" Harper said. "Join you — ?"

"I'd enjoy it, Sheriff," Buchanan said, rising. "Thank you." Lime led the way back to his table. Harper tugged at Buchanan's sleeve, whispered to him urgently.

"What's going on? What's this all about?"

"Sounds like a free drink," Buchanan answered. "You said your luck was high tonight."

"I know, but —"

"Hello, Tom," Cristy said warmly.

148

"Hello, Cristy. I see you made a trade for the shirt and pants."

"No, not a trade. I kept them in case I go riding with a gentleman again. Won't you sit down?"

Buchanan introduced her to the wide-eyed gambler and all three men took chairs around the table. Lime ordered brandy and then turned to Buchanan.

"Cristina has told me your real purpose in Brownsville," he said in a less formal voice. "I admire it, Buchanan, up to a certain point."

"What point is that?"

"I enforce the law here. I am the constituted authority. You are not."

"That's right, Sheriff. On the other hand, I'm not here to enforce any law. I just want to settle an account with three back-shooters."

"You're seeking justice," Lime said, the neat gold star on his vest glistening softly in the candlelight. "That is my department in Brownsville. Which is beside the point, actually."

"How do you mean?"

"It's my opinion that those three men are members of the Leech Gang. You won't find them in town."

"Where will I find them?"

"In a hacienda Leech is using for a temporary headquarters. And to ride out there would be foolhardy, to say the least. Leech has nearly forty men with him, every one of the a professional gunman and killer."

"I'm not looking for every one," Buchanan said mildly. "Just three."

"They're a close-knit outfit, Buchanan," the lawman said. "That's been Leech's main strength for years along the border. Frankly, I wouldn't relish going after them with my own force. Not unless I commanded forty riders and didn't have to attack them in their lair."

The brandies arrived. Cristy leaned forward toward Buchanan.

"John is speaking good sense to you, Tom. I wish you'd heed it — and the advice I gave you about pressing your luck."

"I thank you both," Buchanan said, raising his glass in a toast. "And though nobody here knew him like I did, I'd like to drink a toast to my friend and partner Rig Bogan."

They all four sipped of their glasses.

"Is that your answer?" Cristy asked him.

Buchanan looked to John Lime.

"What is this headquarters for?"

"The merchants here — the exporters — feel that the Mexican custom officials are oppressing them. They've decided on a massive reprisal and hired Leech's so-called army to help them."

"Massive reprisal? You mean smuggling?"

Lime smiled. "As a law officer, Buchanan, I could hardly have knowledge of any smuggling and not report it to a higher authority. This is a reprisal action, undertaken unofficially by private citizens. Men, incidentally, of the highest standing and best reputation."

"When does their smuggling come off?"

Lime frowned. "Their free-trade venture will begin very soon. It's one of the conditions I laid down."

"And where did you say this Leech bunch hangs out?"

"Don't tell him, John!" Cristy said, and Lime's frown deepened at the girl's impulsive concern.

"Don't intend to," he said. "I've been compelled to send fools to the gallows. I would never direct one to his own suicide."

Buchanan tossed off the rest of his brandy, pushed his chair back.

"Thanks again, Sheriff," he said, getting to his feet. He grinned down at Cristy. "I hope the hours suit you better in Brownsville, ma'am," he told her politely.

"I'm sure they will," she said. "But isn't it past your bedtime? The sun has been down for hours."

"This, I suppose, is a private joke," Lime said edgily.

Buchanan turned the grin on him. "Yes, sir," he said, "it is." He swung away from

151

the table, walked out of the place with Hal Harper dogging his heels like a terrier.

"Why didn't you tell me you knew that girl?" the gambler demanded when they were on the boardwalk.

"Don't recall that you asked."

"There's something between you two. What is it?"

Buchanan laughed at the other man's eagerness.

"What would you say if I told you we slept together the last two nights?" he asked mischievously.

"I'd say you were lying or dreaming," Harper answered. "Or both."

"And if I said she makes her living the same way you do — betting suckers they can't make twenty-one?"

"I'd know you were lying."

"Right," Buchanan said. "Listen, do you know where this hacienda is located?"

"Where that wild bunch is? Sure. It's out on the old Wagon Road, about five miles. But you ain't going to let me down tonight, are you? I mean, you're paid in advance and all."

"I'm bought and paid for," Buchanan assured him.

"Whew! Let's get down to the Crystal Palace then and see if this is really my night to howl." They started walking toward the bright lights of the casino section when Harper spoke up again. "Seriously," he said, "did you really sleep with that queen?"

"No.

"Where did you meet her, then?"

"In a little town north of here."

"What was she doing?"

"She was dealing blackjack," Buchanan said. "Like I told you."

Harper looked up at him. "Now," he said, "I don't know what to believe."

Buchanan put a hand on the gambler's shoulder. "Just believe this about Cristy Ford: you met a real fine person tonight."

They entered the Crystal Palace.

NINE

JOHN LIME HAD been obtuse when he said he knew Hal Harper by reputation. In plain fact he knew everything about the dealer that he possibly could learn, and about everyone else who worked in the Crystal Palace — from the chief cashier to the third porter — because the sheriff of Brownsville was not a partner in the city's most profitable gambling house. He owned it outright.

It was a spacious place, with a domed ceiling that muted the noise, crystal chandeliers that hung from solid silver chains, deep carpeting on the oaken floor, a forty-foot by eight-foot oil painting behind the bar that depicted the epochal meeting of Diana and Apollo in some Olympian glen, and a dozen equally voluptuous real-life Dianas who brought liquid refreshments to the gamblers at the tables and were not available — professionally — for anything else.

For John Lime, too, had been in New Orleans, and San Francisco, and Chicago and New York. And if he tried to bring the

154

sophistication and refinement of those cos-
mopolitan cities to the rough and rowdy
border town of Brownsville he could only
be blamed for just that — trying. You could
import the best of everything into Brownsville but you had to take what humans
happened to come your way.

As a result, the Crystal Palace presented
a strange mixture of exotic, high-minded
decor inhabited by a breed of rough-spo-
ken, hard-handed, free-wheeling gambling
men who appreciated nothing more in life
so much as an ace in the hole. Oh, they
looked at Diana on the wall and marveled
at her monumental charms. And guessed
at the cost of the chandeliers. And, by and
large, accepted the chastity of the hostesses
as inviolable. But unlike their gentler breth-
ren in other towns, they made no bones
about the fact that their main purpose
inside the Crystal Palace was to gamble and
win money.

Which John Lime came to understand,
and accept — along with his percentage of
all the money dropped at the tables — as
did Hal Harper, who sincerely appreciated
the attempt that had been made to give the
Crystal Palace tone.

Harper, as he led Buchanan through the
gambling casino to his own table, mentioned the various appointments with a
kind of personal pride.

"Them chandeliers come from Italy," he said. "Direct copies of the exact thing in the palace ballroom. How much you think they cost?"

"Plenty," Buchanan said.

"Five thousand per," Harper said. "And there's twelve of 'em. How do you like that painting?"

"Big," Buchanan said.

"Biggest one behind any bar in the world. And oil, too. I got up there one morning and felt it by hand. All bumpy-like. The real thing."

"Sure is big," Buchanan said.

"You feel that rug under your feet? That's one hundred and fifty separate carpets all sewn together. Goes clear from one wall to the other. Look down. Can you tell where it was sewed?"

"Nope."

"You got to get on your hands and knees, in the daylight. I mean, that's first class."

They came, at last, to where he worked, a rectangular table with chairs for six players on one side and a curved-out slot on the other for himself.

"A lot of money went into this place," Harper said, shedding his coat and high-crowned hat. "And I want to warn you about one thing."

"What's that?"

"Don't make a pass at the girls when they

come around. It's a house rule."

"I'll watch it," Buchanan promised.

"Look 'em over, though," Harper said. "If you see one you like I'll fix it up for you." He winked. "I got connections," he said.

"I'll bet."

Two men came up to the table then, their faces serious, took chairs without a word of greeting and sat there waiting. A colored boy appeared, holding two decks of cards, and threw them atop the felt-topped table.

"Would you open one of those, mister, and count 'em?" Harper said casually. "Like to have a man pick his own poison."

As the man unwrapped the fresh deck Buchanan drifted unobtrusively backward, lowered his big frame into one of the spectator seats nearby. He glanced then at Harper, who shook his head to tell him neither of these was the one he was worried about.

Play began, for token stakes, and though one of the bettors began to win, Harper held his losses to a minimum by scoring against the other. The winner, after twenty minutes, upped the value of his cards to two dollars, doubling the amount whenever he was dealt an ace. And, as Buchanan had been expecting he would, Harper began to concentrate a little more deliberately on that man's layout and to change his tactics. It was, of course, the old come-on. The dealer begins the game in a wild fashion, taking unlikely risks and going over twenty-one himself more often than not. And instead of noting the dealer's chance-taking, the opponent too often credits his own skillful play for his winnings. He doubles his bets, as this one did, and anticipates a killing. Abruptly, the game changes pace. The dealer no longer takes new cards for himself like a bear in a honey barrel. He begins to stand pat on sixteen, even fourteen, and unless his opponent really has Lady Luck standing behind his chair, the old law of averages catches him. Now his game becomes the wild one and he doubles the bet again to recoup. Good money chasing bad, and it all has a way of winding up beside the dealer's elbow.

Another player joined the game, and a fourth, but still no warning signal from Harper. The blackjack game droned on — exciting enough when you're playing but deadly dull to watch. At least it was for Buchanan, who by this time had figured the gambler's style, observed enough small mannerisms to believe that he could give him a lively time across the table. That, however, didn't seem very sporting, somehow. To beat Harper using the man's own twenty-five dollars for a stake . . .

There was a stir nearby and Buchanan looked to see that John Lime had included the Crystal Palace in Cristy's tour of the city. He smiled at the look of surprise the girl feigned as the sheriff demonstrated how a roulette wheel worked, and the birdcage dice, and explained the meaning of all the numbers painted on the side of the big craps table. Slowly they were working their way in his direction and Buchanan was curious to hear what Lime was going to tell her about blackjack.

Hal Harper, in their honor, interrupted his game, rose from the slot and bowed politely. The other players followed suit.

"Perhaps Miss Ford would like to play a few hands?" Harper suggested

"You mean — gamble?" Cristy said, so convincingly that Harper threw Buchanan an accusing look.

"Go on, Cristina," Lime said. "You might find it diverting."

"Oh, but I couldn't. Really —"

"Of course you can, my dear," Lime insisted, taking a wallet from his coat and extracting a fifty dollar bill. "You just sit there and I'll explain how to play."

Cristy's eyes, by force of habit, followed the course of the bill across the table with hawklike interest.

"Fifty ones?" Harper asked, preparing to break it. "Or ten fives?"

"Five tens," Lime told him. "We'll give you a run for it."

"John, really, I couldn't," Cristy was still protesting demurely when her glance happened to lock with Buchanan's. He was grinning at her from ear to ear. She turned her face to Lime. "All right," she said. "If you insist." She sat down in the chair opposite the slot and the play began. Buchanan edged closer to the table, remained standing to get a full view of what was going to happen here. By mutual consent it was to be just she and Harper.

On the first face-up card, Cristy was dealt a ninespot. Lime, peering at the hole card, advised her to take another. She did and it was an eight.

"Well, we lose," Lime said, turning the cards over.

"We do?"

"Yes. You see, my dear, there was a five in the hole. That plus the seventeen makes twenty-two, one over the limit."

"Oh, I see," Cristy said.

Harper dealt again, one down, one up. A jack was showing and Lime leaned down to see the other card. He told her to take a third card. She nodded to Harper and he dealt a second jack.

"Well," Lime said, "we lose again. Those two jacks gave us twenty-four."

"Yes," Cristy said sweetly. "I know."

"Just bad luck, that's all," Hal Harper said sympathetically, but only Buchanan could

160

enjoy the true meaning in the girl's expression at the gambler's remark. Bad luck? it said. That was plain stupid playing.

The third hand was dealt. This time the king of hearts was the up card. Lime took his peek at the hidden one.

"This time, my dear, we'll play these."

"No, John, let's try one more."

"But —"

"One more, please," Cristy said firmly.

"Better listen to Mr. Lime," Harper said. "He knows this game like an expert."

"Another card," Cristy said. "Please."

Harper shrugged, peeled the card from the top of the deck. It was an eight, making a total of eighteen showing, and Harper actually looked like he was sorry he'd won.

But had he?

"Now we have enough," Cristy was saying. "Don't you think so, John?"

"Yes, my dear," Lime said, his voice admiring.

"Now it's your turn, Mr. Harper, isn't it?" Cristy said with an innocent smile.

"It sure is," Harper replied. His up card was the jack and now he looked to see what he had in the hole. "The dealer takes another," he announced. It was the four of clubs. "All right, Miss," he said. "The dealer pays twenty."

"Why, that's just what we have, isn't it, John?" And she did, eighteen up and a twospot under. Cristy won the fourth hand, the fifth and the sixth, each time gently but firmly overruling Lime's "expert" advice. Harper had just begun dealing the seventh round when there was an objection raised in a surly, ill-tempered voice.

"Whatta you doin', dealer?" Jules Perrott snarled. "Tryin' to cut me out because I got your number?" He pulled a chair out, sat down in it defiantly, and Buchanan didn't need any signal from Harper to know that this raw-boned, tough talking new-comer was the one he'd been hired to han-dle. He shifted his position so that he was behind the slot.

"Deal me in, small man," Perrott de-manded. "I bet a hundred."

John Lime walked to where he was seated. "There are other tables where you can play blackjack," he said to him. "Go find yourself one."

Perrott surveyed the other man with an insolent leer, paid particular attention to the fact that Lime had come out for a social evening unarmed.

"I like it right here, dude," he said. "And tonight I'm gonna break this game for good."

"I'm ordering you to move," Lime said tightly. "In fact, I'm ordering you out of this casino altogether." Perrott laughed up at him, slid his hand back along his belt to the protruding gunbutt. Lime turned half-way around, searching for a deputy.

Buchanan had quit watching the argument a moment before. He was looking down at Cristy, reading the expression of startled concern in her beautiful face. He glanced sharply at the newcomer again, took a step to his left that put the length of the table between them.

Perrott had laughed in John Lime's face, moved his long fingers to the .44. "Whatta you mean, you're orderin'," he asked menacingly. "Nobody orders me —"

"Stand up, mister," Buchanan's voice said, cracking like a whip. The seated man switched his attention swiftly. "Are you Gill?" Buchanan asked. "Or Perrott?"

"What's it to you?"

"Gill or Perrott?" Buchanan repeated.

"I'm Jules Perrott! So what?"

"Mr. Lime," Buchanan said, "take Cristy out of the way. Harper, the rest of you — back off."

"No, Tom!" Cristy cried out.

"Get her out of the way," Buchanan said again, his wintry gaze boring into Perrott's face. Lime pulled the girl from the chair, moved her aside. Hal Harper and the other players jumped clear.

"Say, boy," Jules Perrott drawled, "what the hell's goin' on here tonight?" He accompanied it with a lazy smile, but his own scowling, deep-set little eyes watched Buchanan intently.

"A shiny new red wagon," Buchanan said. "The Double-B Fast Freight. Remember it?"

"Maybe."

"A 'B' for Bogan and a 'B' for Buchanan. I'm Buchanan —"

Jules Perrott fired without leaving his seat. Fired through an open-end swivel holster that he kept greased for times just like this. That sneak shot was his favorite, and there wasn't a man in Leech's gang who wasn't wary of him for it. Perrott fired through the holster and then did leave his seat. He was blown clear out of the chair by a slug from Buchanan's Colt that caught him almost dead center. Off center about one-sixteenth of an inch. Buchanan hit him with two more before the man's body had reached the carpeted floor, then swung around, searchingly.

"*Fred* Perrott, you here?" he called out to the stunned room. "Are you here, *Sam Gill?* Now's your chance, boys!"

They weren't present and Buchanan holstered the smoking .45 until the next time. That was the signal that released the onlookers.

"Jeezu!" Hal Harper breathed for them all. "I'll tell the world you can use that thing!"

John Lime agreed, was impressed, but the

thin-skinned and position-conscious sheriff was having some immediate second thoughts on what had occurred and he didn't like at all the role in which he'd been cast. He could hear Buchanan ordering him around, relegating him to shepherd, to common spectator. And not only in front of this impressionable crowd but before the eyes of the young lady he, himself, was trying to impress. Second best was not for John Lime, and now he acted impulsively to regain face.

"Buchanan!"

Buchanan turned, his eyes quizzical at the stern tone.

"I warned you," Lime said, "about taking the law into your own hands. You deliberately provoked that gunplay just now."

Buchanan smiled sheepishly. "Damn near provoked myself to death," he admitted. "Them swivel jobs are tricky —"

"You're under arrest, Buchanan!"

"John," Cristy said, "you're not serious?"

"Please don't interfere, Cristina. The law has been broken. There can be no compromise with justice. Not in my town." He moved away from her, came to stand directly before Buchanan. "Hand me your gun, Buchanan."

Buchanan looked down, half-smiling, half-squinting.

"I don't get you, Mr. Lime," he said softly.

"What harm's been done to your precious law?"

"I said hand me your gun. You're under arrest."

Buchanan looked over the man's head, into Cristy's eyes, Hal Harper's, glanced at the faces of total strangers. In each he saw the same disturbance he was feeling, the bewilderment, the inability to comprehend Lime's position. And, importantly, Buchanan felt their oneness with him, their complete support if he defied the sheriff, told him to go to hell. Even Cristy.

His eyes went again to Lime's intense, unyielding expression and the urge was there, all right, to brush the sanctimonious little martinet aside and be on his way.

"For the third and last time, Buchanan, your gun!"

The candlelight in the crystal chandelier overhead caught Lime's small gold badge and made it glisten. Not a shield at all like the tarnished, bullet-creased old star that Jess Bogan wore back in Alpine. But they both stood for the same thing, the law, and suddenly the persons of John Lime and Jess Bogan became fused in Buchanan's mind.

He lifted the Colt from its holster backhanded and surrendered it.

"That's showing good sense, mister," Lime said.

"Just take it," Buchanan advised him. "Don't talk about it."

The sheriff of Brownsville followed his big prisoner out of the Crystal Palace, had to quicken his stride to keep pace, and he wondered just how much of his dignity he'd regained.

TEN

IT NEVER OCCURED to Turkey Forbes to report first to Lash Wall. He hurried into the hacienda, stood in the doorway of the room where the poker game was in progress and announced his news in a shrill, charged voice.

"Jules Perrott is dead!"

The roomful of gunmen seemed to freeze, then one by one they all swung their attention to Fred Perrott. Perrott's slack jaw hung open as he slowly climbed to his feet.

"Say that again," he said hollowly.

"Your brother just got himself shot and killed in Brownsville," Forbes repeated. "I couldn't follow what him and the big guy was arguin' about, but it sure got over in a hurry."

"How big?" Wynt Jenkins asked.

"Near as big as Big Red."

"Ain't nobody as big as me!" Leech himself said loudly, coming into the room. He glanced around at the faces of his men. "What's the matter here?"

"Somebody got Jules Perrott," Sherm Moore informed him.

"Got him?" Leech echoed. "Who? Where?"

"He slipped into town tonight," Turkey Forbes said. "Lash sent me to keep an eye on him. Only I was too late. It was all over before it started, seemed like."

"You were there," Fred Perrott said, "and didn't take a hand?"

"Listen, Fred," Forbes answered, "that fella spotted your brother that swivel shot of his and plugged him three times through the heart. Then he swings the gun around and starts callin' for fresh meat — namely you and Sam Gill."

"He knew us?" the heavy-set Gill asked.

Forbes shook his head. "It wasn't like he *knew* you, Sam. Just your name, and Fred's. And he invited you both to step up and try him."

"Well, I'll damn well oblige him," Fred Perrott said, stepping forward. "Come on, Sam."

Lash Wall had come into the room, heard a part of the conversation.

"Hold on, Fred," he said.

"Hold on, hell! Jules is dead."

"If it's the ramstam I think it is," Wynt Jenkins drawled, "you and Sam better approach him real careful."

"Amen," Sherm Moore said dryly.

"You mean the same one that took Prado and you?" Lash Wall asked.

"The description is close," Wynt replied.

"Especially the spotting old Jules' first shot, then hitting him three times."

"He don't scare me none," Fred Perrott said hotly. "Stand aside, Lash!"

"Everybody hold on here!" Big Red thundered. "Who's runnin' this outfit, anyhow?"

"Big Red, somebody is cutting this outfit down," Lash Wall commented. "We can't lose any more."

"Don't tell me what we can and can't!" Leech shouted at his lieutenant. "Now, forgettin' the fact that Jules disobeyed me personal, the fact remains that there's some scudder runnin' around loose and makin' this army look bad. We got hired for this job on our rep, and by damn I ain't gonna lose it to no lucky shootin' sonofabitch! Saddle up, everybody!" Leech ordered. "We got a maverick in Brownsville that needs lynchin'!"

"He's already in the pokey, Red," Turkey Forbes announced. "The sheriff took him in immediate for shootin' Jules."

"Then we'll just take him the hell out of the pokey!"

"No, Big Red," Lash Wall protested. "That sheriff will fight —"

"Hope he does! What's gettin' into you, Lash? Losin' your nerve?"

"My nerve is the same as ever, Big Red. What you're losing are the boys we need to

170

get this job done!"

"Then to hell with the job!" Leech roared down at him. "The rep of this outfit comes first with me! Let's go, boys!"

"Down!" John Lime commanded the trio of chained, snarling, hungry-looking bull mastiffs that guarded his jail. *"Down!"* he snapped, and the half-wild beasts obeyed, reluctantly, casting aggressive glances at Buchanan as they slunk into the shadows. The jail itself was nothing more than an out-sized adobe hut, with a portal instead of a door, partitions rather than cells and narrow slit windows without bars. John Lime lit a lantern that rested on a scarred table just inside the portal, sending a huge rat scurrying into its nest beneath the cracked floor, throwing light on a tarantula who had complete possession of one entire ceiling corner. Inside each partitioned section was a mattress of straw that looked as old as the building itself.

"Some calaboose," Buchanan commented.

"I don't believe in fancy jails," Lime said.

"Guess you don't."

"Nor in taking prisoners. Waste of good money."

Buchanan looked at him. "You got me for a prisoner," he said.

"Temporarily," Lime said.

"Oh, yeah?"

Lime shook his head. "Nothing like that," he said. "I'm going to send a deputy around with your belongings and your horse. He'll escort you out of Brownsville, Buchanan, and you'll keep right on going."

"You're sure positive about things, aren't you?" Buchanan asked him, feeling his irritation rising to an active level again.

"Very positive," the lawman said and then his features seemed to relent in the lantern's flickering glow. "I have to be, Buchanan," he said. "I couldn't be any other way and still maintain law and order in this border city. If I showed one sign of weakness, of indecision, Brownsville would turn on me the same as those dogs out front." The man sighed, smiled curiously. "It's not easy," he said, "being John Lime."

"Why do you keep at it?" Buchanan asked him.

Lime kept smiling, gave a shrug of his shoulders beneath the expensive coat. "Some men are born to hold power," he said in a different voice. "They are put on earth to direct the lives of lesser men, to run things. I happen to be one of those chosen." He sighed again, shook his head. "But it's a lonely road to travel. Lonely and friendless." His eyes seemed to focus sharply on Buchanan's face. "I envy a man like you," Lime said. "You don't know how lucky you are."

"Yeah," the tall man said, looking around at his doleful surroundings. "This is the high life."

"I also like you," Lime said surprisingly. "I almost wish I didn't have to send you on your way."

"Oh, I'll be right back," Buchanan told him.

"You'll *what?*"

"Be back," Buchanan repeated. "I figure the brother and his sidekick'll show up now. Wouldn't want to miss 'em."

"I just said that I liked you, Buchanan," John Lime said, his voice and manner withdrawn again. "But I'm ordering you out of the territory. Defy me and the consequences will be very serious. Very," he added and moved toward the open portal. "I'll send a man to ride you out of Brownsville," he said then. "Don't force me to do anything more." He stepped out into the darkness and was gone. Immediately, the dogs set up a vicious clamor, strained fiercely at their chains to get at the prisoner inside the miserable jail.

Buchanan eyed his lively guards from the entranceway, speculating wryly that they added a certain extra hazard if a man had escape on his mind.

"Nice little doggies," he called out to them,

experimentally, but the sound of his voice only increased their frenzy. Just plain un-friendly, he decided, and tried no more overtures. Fifteen minutes went by, twenty, then half an hour passed without a sign of the deputy Lime had promised. Finally a rider appeared in the street outside, trailing Buchanan's filly behind him.

"You in there, buddy?" the deputy called.

"I ain't out for a stroll," Buchanan assured him. "What kept you?"

"I'll tell you what kept me, this goddamn ornery horse of yours kept me! Liked to have stomped me to death tryin' to get the bit in her mouth!"

"She's stealproof," Buchanan explained. "Has to know a man for a spell."

"Even got my stallion jittery," the man complained, dismounting. "God help any stud takes a notion to her."

"She'll pick one out when she's ready," Buchanan said, watching the deputy make a wary approach. "You know them dogs real well?" he asked him.

"I know 'em, all right. Sometimes they forget they know me."

"All Lime said was down," Buchanan told him helpfully.

"That's Lime," the man outside replied. "I happen to be named Boyd. Generally," he added, "if I stand here till they get my scent they let me by. Takes a minute or so,

174

depending on how hungry they are."

"They ain't fed since Christmas from the sound of 'em," Buchanan said, not noticing any letup in their snarling and growling.

"Down!" the deputy ordered, but without Lime's bland assurance of being obeyed. "Back off there, Leo! Down, King! Down, Vixen!" The three animals abated some, seemed confused for a moment. Deputy Boyd kept talking to them, edged forward, and the dogs finally decided to let him walk past. He stopped at the portal.

"Let them see me takin' hold of your arm," he said to Buchanan. "That usually works."

"Usually?"

"More times than not," Boyd amended.

"Well, just in case," Buchanan said, "let me have my Colt back."

"To shoot Lime's dogs? Mister, you must be out of your head —" His voice broke off at the sound of his name being called from up the street.

"Boyd!" John Lime shouted, his voice erratic. "Hold the prisoner in there!"

Now what? Buchanan thought, his patience thin. Lime appeared before the jail, followed by half a dozen of his men. They all carried rifles and seemed agitated. Lime strode past his dogs as though they weren't there.

"You've apparently stirred the hornets," he said to Buchanan. "Red Leech is looking for you with his entire crew."

"Well, thanks, Sheriff, for the tip," Buchanan said and started around the man. Lime got in his way.

"Where do you think you're going?"

"Going out," Buchanan told him. "Man's a sitting duck in here."

"Sorry about that, Buchanan," Lime said, "but you're in my custody. How would I look if I set you free now? Everyone would accuse me of sidestepping a threat from this arrogant bandit —"

Buchanan looked his amazement. "You told me he's got six guns to your one," he said, trying to keep his tone reasonable. "You take a fight like that out into the open country, whittle him down to size. Man, you don't sit in a damn chicken coop and wait for him to take you."

"We disagree," Lime said, and even as he spoke the clamor sounded. There were many riders coming this way, coming nearer by the moment. Lime turned to Deputy Boyd, lifted the Colt from the man's belt and returned it to Buchanan. "Defend yourself," he said. "We're in this together."

It was the damnedest fool thing Buchanan had ever heard of. Foolish, but beyond the arguing stage now. Leech's army had arrived outside, were forming a tight, ominous-looking ring around the adobe jail. The dogs set up a fierce din.

"This the hoosegow?" Red Leech roared above their racket.

"This is my jail, Leech!" Lime called back. "And you're off limits! Turn around and get back where you belong!"

"Why sure, brother, sure! Soon's we stretch that ranny's neck for ya!"

"The man is my prisoner," Lime told him. "He's under no sentence to hang!"

"I say different!" Leech bellowed. "Push him out here by the count of three or I'll blow this pokey over! Start the count, Perrott!"

"One!" Fred Perrott shouted, and from inside the building Buchanan tried to make out the man and the direction of his voice.

"Two!"

"Last chance, by God!" Leech warned.

"THREE!"

Thirty-five handguns thundered with one deafening voice. Slugs screamed through the portal in front, through the slit windows in back, crashed against the four walls and rocked the little building visibly.

The defenders answered back, but not with that tremendous firepower, that overwhelming impact. Buchanan, with single-minded devotion to his mission in Brownsville, knelt in the opening and sighted carefully on the rider who had tolled the count. Once, twice, three times he punished Fred Perrott for the cowardly murder of Rig Bogan and consigned him to hell. And, on either side of him, two of Lime's men went down.

"Pour it on!" Leech bawled and another volley slammed against the doomed jailhouse, inside and out. A jagged section of the back wall fell in. Only four of the trapped guns replied, and one of those silenced was Lime himself. Buchanan pulled the fallen lawman away from the portal.

"Hit bad?" he asked him.

"In the forearm. Fractured the bone, I think."

"Give 'em hell!" Leech cried at the top of his lungs and the third round racketed relentlessly. One more of Lime's deputies screamed and fell. Another went down without a murmur and lay still.

"I seemed to have made a mistake," Lime murmured through his pain. "Should have listened. Fought them in the open —"

"Hold your fire, boys!" Leech ordered outside. "All right, in there!" he called. "Anybody wants to come out, he's got a ten-second truce! Startin' now!"

"You two," Buchanan said to the remaining deputies. "Pick up your boss and get out of here. Quick!"

They nodded, unafraid but grateful, lifted John Lime gently between them and carried him outside, past the bodies of his three jailguards who had died in the first barrage.

"Who else?" Leech shouted into the tense quiet. "Time's up!"

Buchanan had gone to the damaged back wall, was testing the gaping hole with his fingers.

"*You asked for it!*" Leech bellowed and Buchanan hit the wall with his big shoulder in the same instant. The old mortar gave way with a groan, giving the man an exit that caught the gunmen at the rear of the building by surprise.

"*Fire!*" Leech was bawling out front and the blast of his guns was instantaneous. But Buchanan was running at right angles to the building, low and fast. He was spotted in the bright orange gunflashes.

"Somebody gettin' away, Red!"

"That's him!" Turkey Forbes yelled piercingly. "That's the scudder kilt Jules!"

"Get the son!" Big Red Leech thundered. "Ride the bastard down!"

The fox and the hounds. Buchanan plunged on into the darkness, and as unnatural as it felt to run out on an argument the tall man adapted himself to the situation with such gusto as to make himself wonder how his Highland ancestors had made their living.

He took his pursuers west for fifty yards, directly into a thick cluster of shacks and stores that was the marketplace of the

179

Mexican section, then led Leech's Gang through a maze of narrow streets and alleyways toward the slaughterhouses, where a hundred busy men labored at their butchering by torchlight and a thousand head of cattle bawled dolorously in their pens. Leech's men suddenly found themselves on skittish, unwilling horses — animals with the scent of fresh blood in their sensitive nostrils and no desire to come any closer.

That was Buchanan's pure luck, not design. In fact, he could have stayed in the neighborhood indefinitely, but now he changed direction, went south to the riverfront, slid down the black, sloping bank of the Rio and caught himself a second breath. He could hear Leech and company thrashing around in the night, making a great commotion, but no one came within three hundred feet of his hiding place.

Then the noises died down, the pursuit was abandoned, and a frustrated, bad-tempered Red Leech turned his crew back to the hacienda. Lash Wall, his own temper simmering close to the surface, pulled abreast of the massive, bearded man.

"Well?" Wall asked curtly, "what did this night accomplish?"

Leech, stung, swung his head sharply.

"We give that high-and-mighty sheriff a lickin', didn't we?" he demanded. "Showed him what we can do, by damn!"

"And lost Fred Perrott, which we couldn't afford."

"Why the hell don't you whistle another tune?" Leech snarled at him.

Wall lapsed into silence, retreated into the fortress of his mind. He was, he knew, dangerously close to an open breach with Big Red. For a long time now the other man's loud voice and high-handed manner had chafed, made his resentment grow. And with each passing day it was becoming more and more clear to Lash Wall that Red Leech had neither the ability nor the ambition to realize what could be done in this raw, disorganized country with a private army such as this one.

This raid on the jail tonight was a case in point. Wall had given a lot of quiet thought to the setup John Lime had in Brownsville. He had also come to the conclusion that, at the proper time, Lime could be taken. But not tonight. Tonight they should have stayed at the headquarters, saved their energy and their enthusiasm for the big job tomorrow. As it stood now they had accomplished nothing with this raid except to be one valuable gun shy for the operation. And if Lime had not chosen to coop himself up in that building they would surely have lost more. Just as serious, Lime was on his guard now. The sheriff would be waiting for them next time, in force, and the price for taking over rich Brownsville would be ten times as expensive.

All because this big blowhard riding next to him had to protect his reputation. Which he hadn't, because the man they had come to town for was still on the loose. Still loose, and apparently with some score still to be settled with Sam Gill.

What the hell was that all about, anyhow? He pulled his horse up, let Leech move ahead, and when he spotted Gill's blocky, stolid-looking figure among the body of riders, he eased in beside the man.

"How you feeling, Sam?"

"I could use a drink," Gill answered gruffly. He didn't like Lash Wall especially and the feeling was mutual. Sam Gill didn't like a great many men, and that was mutual, too.

"Tough break for Fred tonight," Wall said.

"Yeah."

"Bad night for Perrotts all around."

"Yeah."

"What's this gent so burry about, Sam? What'd you and Fred and Jules do to him?"

Gill looked at Wall for the first time. "Ask Fred and Jules," he said. "Me, I wouldn't know."

"Some husband, maybe? A brother?"

"I said, Lash, I wouldn't know."

"You have any trouble like that up in Uvalde?" Wall persisted.

"What the hell is it to you what we had in Uvalde?"

"I'll tell you what it is to me, Sam," Wall said calmly. "I pulled this crew together very carefully, handpicked every man for the biggest job that ever came our way. As of tonight I count three dead and one who can't work his gun. One man did all that, Sam, and I'd like to know what's biting him."

"I wouldn't know," Gill said again.

"But you do know you're on his list?"

"If I'm on anybody's *list*," Gill said, "I'll take care of it myself. Don't you worry about me."

"I'm not, Sam," Lash Wall told him. "It's your gun I'm worried about." He parted company from the truculent man, pushed on up to the front of the pack.

What was it all about? he wondered still. What had Sam Gill and the Perrotts done?

Sam Gill, Buchanan was thinking at that very moment. He had climbed up from the riverbank, duly grateful for the refuge it had given him but feeling unnatural in his mind just the same for having been chased into hiding.

Sam Gill, he thought as he traced his way back past the slaughterhouse and reached the scene of the lopsided battle at the jail. There was activity of another kind there now, of mercy and sorrow. An ambulance and several other wagons were drawn up before the battered building, half-a-hundred citizens of Brownsville milled around in the bright light of as many torches.

Buchanan borrowed one, went looking for his horse and came upon her grazing imperturbably in a field a quarter mile away. He checked the filly carefully, found her unmarked, lifted himself onto her back and took her back to the jail.

John Lime, his own arm in a makeshift bandage and sling, was directing the removal of his men. Boyd and another deputy were badly wounded but still alive. The other two were fatalities of Leech's raid.

"Anything I can help with, Sheriff?" Buchanan asked and Lime looked up at the mounted man with a surprised smile.

"I had word they'd caught you," he said. "Down by the river."

"Not yet they didn't. How's the wing?"

"Damned annoying," Lime said, gazing at Buchanan intently. "I have something I want to ask you," he said then. "It may sound rather strange in view of other things that have occurred tonight."

"Ask it."

"How would you like a job? An important one?"

"Doing what?"

"Being my chief deputy," Lime said and

now it was Buchanan's turn to be surprised.

"Strange is right, Sheriff."

"Well, man, how about it?"

Buchanan shook his head. "That's out of my line," he said. "Sitting around an office all day playing checkers, pulling in drunks and stopping fights all night."

"There's a lot more to law enforcement than that," Lime said, his voice indignant. "And in Brownsville there's a great future for my chief deputy."

"Thanks for the offer," Buchanan said, "but it's not for me."

"Will you do this — will you think it over tonight? Give me your final answer in the morning?"

"All right, Sheriff, if you'll do me a little favor."

"Name it."

"Tell me where the old Wagon Road is from here."

"The Wagon Road? Why, that runs out that way, due west. What do you want —" He broke off, frowning. "You're not seriously thinking of going out there after them?"

"Just one," Buchanan answered. "Name of Gill."

"I see. And you'll simply knock on the front door and tell them to send Gill out."

"Something like that."

"And Gill, of course, will just hand himself over to you."

"No," Buchanan said. "I expect he'll argue some."

"You're damn well told he will! And he'll have every one of his hardcase friends to back him up."

"Excepting two," Buchanan said, smiling as he swung the filly around. *"Hasta,"* he called back to the other man as he rode away west.

Rode steadily but unhurriedly, reminding himself that there was no special rush now. Sam Gill would be waiting for him.

The hacienda loomed large and graceful and was ablaze with light. Buchanan took a full turn around the place, studying the physical layout, observing the actvity within the walls. There were men moving around on the second floor, talking and drinking, and others were gathered in a big room below, some playing poker, some watching.

Just a bunch of boys in a bunkhouse, Buchanan thought, then chuckled aloud. Some fancy bunkhouse.

In the right wing of the second floor he saw two men seated at a table in earnest conversation. One had a thick beard and a long mane of hair, reddish-hued even from out here in the dark, and he had his big hand wrapped around a whisky bottle. One moment he gesticulated with it, shook it in the other man's face, and the next he pulled at the neck. The other man was slender and cleanshaven — and listening.

Red Leech, Buchanan decided, dismounting. He slid the Winchester from its boot, levered the rifle and then settled down to a prone position behind a small hillock, shifting his hips and elbows into the soft ground until he was comfortable.

Then he blasted the bottle out of Red Leech's fingers.

All they could do — Leech and Lash Wall — was stare at the jagged glass, its top half still dripping whisky onto the floor. Wall recovered first.

"It's him," he said.

"What?"

"Him," Wall repeated, unshocked enough to turn down the wick in the lantern, uncertain about dimming the light across the room. "He's after Sam Gill."

Red Leech flung the neck of the whisky bottle back through the shattered window, stood up furiously.

"Well, goddamn it, I ain't Sam Gill!" he roared out into the night. And dropping to all fours as the rifle out there all but parted his hair.

"Sonofabitch," Red Leech said from the

floor, chastened. "We got to put a stop to that mutt."

"It'll cost us before we do," Lash Wall pointed out.

Down below, the crack of the first shot had caused some confusion among the poker players. The second sent them scurrying for guns and cover. One man, Frank Hancock, had just drawn a third queen to a full house and his anger at the interruption outweighed his discretion. He pushed open the window, raised his .44, and was promptly brought to his senses by a pair of screaming 30-30 slugs past either ear.

Some of the besieged inmates got off angry answering shots from various parts of the big house, but by and large Buchanan kept objections down with his pinpoint fire. Their disadvantage, he well knew, was in trying to decide whether they were escaping death by luck or if the sniper was missing on purpose.

He watched with interest as the room on the first floor emptied out and a conference began to take place on the floor above. One would-be hero didn't attend the meeting, tried to sneak out of the house. The 30-30 kicked up dust at his boots, drove him back inside again.

The conference looked to Buchanan to be a personal argument between Leech and the other fellow. Finally a vote was taken, on something, and the cleanshaven man seemed to have won his point by an overwhelming show of hands. A minute later the main door was opened and a flag of truce appeared.

"How about a parley, friend?" Lash Wall called out into the dark.

"Sure, friend," Buchanan answered genially.

"I'm leaving my gun inside," Wall promised. "I'm coming out without it."

"Come any damn way you please," Buchanan advised him.

Wall stepped from the big house and his heels clicked sharply as he crossed the flagstone courtyard, seemed extra loud because it was the only sound there was. Watchful faces began to appear in the windows behind him.

"This way," Buchanan said, getting up slowly, keeping a prvdent eye out for any treachery from some other direction. Not too worried, though. There had been a note of sincerity in the voice of the man approaching him. Then he and Lash Wall were facing each other.

"Wall's my name."

"I'm Buchanan."

"And damned handy with that rifle," Lash said dryly.

"She's a Winchester," Buchanan said, as if that explained his shooting.

"Well," Wall said, putting an end to the brief amenities, "what can we do for you, Buchanan?"

"I've come for Sam Gill," Buchanan said. "Send him out here."

"Come clear from Uvalde, did you?"

"Uvalde? No."

"You're some kind of law, then? A marshal?"

"No," Buchanan said again. "Not even collecting bounty for the skunk, though I reckon there's some along his back trail."

"Where's your profit, then? What do you want with Gill?"

"Satisfaction, friend. Now go send him out here to me."

"Satisfaction for what? What did Sam and the Perrott brothers do to you, anyhow?"

Buchanan hesitated for a moment, took a deep, troubled sigh and began to speak very quietly. "The three bastards," he said, "dropped some money in a game of blackjack one night. Next morning they followed the winner out of town. They rode up behind him and shot him in the back. They killed this boy, robbed him, destroyed his goods and didn't even have the decency to bury him. Send Sam Gill out here."

Now it was Lash Wall who sighed, whose voice shook when he spoke again.

"This boy was your brother?"

"Just as close to me as one. Rig Bogan

was my partner. Now let's cut the damn palaver. Tell Gill I'll be waiting for him over yonder, back of the caretaker's place."

"All right," Wall said, "I'll tell him." He turned, paused, and looked back for another moment. "Watch yourself real careful, Buchanan," he said. "I hear you spotted Jules Perrott a shot tonight. You can't do that with Sam Gill."

"Thanks for the warning," Buchanan said, and as Wall made his way back to the hacienda the tall man slid the Winchester back in its boot, walked leisurely toward the dark, squat shape of the caretaker's house and the equipment shed adjoining it.

Lash Wall stood before the entire gang assembled upstairs and repeated Buchanan's grievance. He spoke as neutrally as he could manage to, and when he was finished stepped aside. There was a long embarrassed silence before Red Leech, himself, broke it.

"You been called a bushwhacker, Sam. What do you got to say for yourself?" The voice, for Leech, was strangely subdued.

Gill looked around at the familiar faces, his own expression contemptuous, settled his gaze defiantly on Big Red.

"Me and Fred and Jules," he said slowly, "decided we'd been cheated by this freight driver. What we give him was just what every card shark deserves in this country."

"How come you waited till mornin'?" Leech asked. "How come you didn't know you was bein' cheated at the time, Sam?"

"He was too slick, for one," Gill replied offhandedly. "Besides, we'd been drinkin' pretty steady. That cheater took us at an unfair advantage."

"So you and the Perrotts got up next mornin' and took a vote? You voted you'd been slickered. By a freighter, not a tinhorn gambler."

"What the hell is this, Big Red? A trial or somethin'?"

"Or somethin', Sam," Leech told him. "Now about this last thing the fella out there told Lash, about not buryin' this freight driver you bushwhacked. Is that the truth on it, Sam?"

"That's nothin' but rock and hard pan up there!" Gill protested. "Christ almighty, a man'd spend a day diggin' a hole in that land. Besides, what'd we want to bury a damn card cheat for? Leave him rot, I say, as a warnin'!"

Leech had started walking toward him ponderously. Now he stopped.

"I'm a great believer in a man's rep, Sam," he told Gill. "Right now yours is pretty low."

Gill's eyes blazed. "Low, hanh? For riddin' the world of a lousy, wise-crackin' card cheat? Wouldn't bury a goddamn rattler, would you, Big Red?"

"Me," Leech told him, "I say you got to go out there and showdown with this fella. Go get your reputation back." He swung his massive head to the others. "Anybody disagree?"

No one did.

"Sure, sure," Gill said. "Step out the door and let him plug me with that goddamn rifle. What kind of fool do you take me for?"

"He told Lash he'd meet you out by the little shack," Leech said. "Now, I don't know this scudder except for *his* rep. I say he'll be waitin' for you, Sam, where he said he would. Fair and square."

"Easy enough for you to say."

"Sam, you'll go out that door and fight him," Leech said. "Or you'll be carried out on top of that door. Toes up."

There was a stirring in the big room then. Sam Gill knew that he was a minority of one. He raised his head and a broad, confident smirk appeared on his face. His husky shoulders squared.

"All right, Big Red," he said, "I'll go out there and take him. You ever known Sam Gill to back down from a fight?"

"Never."

"Or lose one?"

"Never," Leech said again.

Gill started across the room with an air of bravado, turned in the doorway jauntily.

"Be right back, boys," he said, slipping his .45 from the holster smoothly and checking the load. "Save me a bottle."

They could hear his boots descending the oak stairs to the floor below, a confident sound about them, and they watched from the windows as he walked steadily, without hesitation, across the courtyard.

"Ought to be a good fight," Frank Hancock said. "Anybody want to bet Sam don't take him?"

There were no takers.

Sam Gill crossed the courtyard with the sure, icy confidence of a battle-tested veteran. The gun that rode comfortably on his hip was his living and his life, and he knew exactly how good he was with it. He knew, too, that he was going to the most important fight he had ever had. This kill would raise him head and shoulders above the rest, give him permanent stature in the gang. And erase the stigma laid on him by the bushwhacking charge.

His most important fight, and Gill knew that he was up for it. He could feel it all through his body, feel every nerve alert, pitched to razor sharpness. Even the sound of his steps on the flagstone seemed magnified.

Suddenly he stopped in mid-stride and a smile of cunning appeared slowly on his lips. Why, he wondered, announce his coming?

He lifted one foot, slipped the boot off, did the same with the other and set them both down very quietly. Now he began walking again, as soundless and stealthy as a cat.

Buchanan had been listening to the clicking heels, and when it stopped so abruptly he frowned, wondered if the other man had run out of nerve. Sure sounded cocky enough just a second ago.

He was standing well back from the corner of the house, unprotected by the shadows, determined to give Sam Gill the selfsame chance to kill him as he wanted. But when the silence beyond the house continued, Buchanan began to move slowly in that direction.

He moved that way, and Gill, in stocking feet, circled the little house from the other side, came up at Buchanan's back. Then they were both there, not thirty feet apart, and the only warning Buchanan ever had was the whispery creak of Gill's gun barrel clearing leather.

Two shots murdered the silence all around, close-spaced as two seconds. One of the guns roared a second time, a third. The tumbling echoes of the blasts rolled away and a taut silence descended once again.

Until a tremendous voice shattered it anew.

"Now, goddamn it," bellowed Red Leech, "are you done back there?"

"Done," Buchanan called back softly, the Colt already holstered. He turned from the dead Sam Gill, began to walk away.

"Wait," a voice called and Lash Wall came up to him, his manner eager, his eyes bright even in that darkness. The same darkness that had led Sam Gill into a fatal mistake of judgment. "Wait," Lash Wall said. "Big Red wants to meet you. And I want to have a little more parley." He took Buchanan by the arm, turned him around persuasively, and led him back to the court-yard.

"Shake hands with Buchanan, Big Red," he said.

The two men locked palms, took each other's measure.

"By damn, you are as big as me!" Leech exclaimed. "Almost! You wanna wrestle, brother?"

Buchanan laughed. "No, brother," he told him, "not tonight."

"Tomorra then!" Leech urged. "Man, I ain't tried my bear hug on a fittin' opponent in near a year or more!"

"Ought to keep a few bears handy," Buchanan suggested. Lash Wall stepped closer.

"In case it slipped your mind, Big Red," he said dryly, "tomorrow's when this crew goes back to work."

"Now ain't that hell? All right, brother, we'll lock horns when the job's done! How's that?"

"Occurred to me," Wall said then, "that Buchanan might want to come along and make himself a pile."

Big Red beamed, landed Buchanan a whack on the back that would have driven another man into the ground.

"Great!" Leech roared happily. "Great idea, Lash!"

"Wish I could, boys," Buchanan said. "But I got other plans."

"What other plans?" Leech demanded.

"Going to New Orleans," Buchanan said, speaking as though he really meant it.

"You can go to New Orleans any time, Buchanan," Wall said smoothly. "But you won't fall into a deal like this one very often."

Buchanan shook his head. "Thanks, though, for the offer."

"Don't you think you owe us something?" Wall said.

"*Owe* you?"

"Why, sure," Leech said, scowling fiercely. "You kilt Prado, didn't ya, and laid old Wynt up with a busted collarbone?"

"Plus the Perrotts and Sam Gill," Wall put in.

"That's five good guns I can't use," Leech

197

accused. "Thanks to you!"

"I'm sorry about that," Buchanan said, "but not very."

"Tell you what," Lash Wall said then. "We'll take the one of you for the five of them, pay you full shares on each. That, in case you're curious, comes to fifteen thousand gold dollars."

Buchanan looked down into the man's smiling face, thought about Honest John Magee back up in San Antone. And Banker Penney. And a thousand dollars Rig had wanted to send back to Alpine. Chances were those three men would never get the straight story on what happened to Rig Bogan. The Double-B Fast Freight Company, in fact, would always be a sorry memory to them, under a cloud.

"What do you say?" Wall prodded at him and Buchanan smiled back.

"Suppose," he said, "I was to plug a couple more of your boys. Could you raise the ante then to twenty thousand?"

"Plug a couple more —" Red Leech roared, then got the joke and laughed boisterously. He gave Buchanan another tremendous thump on the back. "Twenty it is, brother!" he said generously. "I'll cut the rest out of Lash's share!"

And Lash Wall made no protest about that, nor the rip-roaring party that followed the hasty, irreverent burial of Sam Gill.

Wall had a hunch that the new addition to the Leech army was the difference between success and failure of the operation. Besides which, he would be handling all the money that came from the merchants and Big Red would never know whose share had been shaved to pay the recruit.

ELEVEN

TWENTY-FOUR HOURS later the three of them sat their horses on the Texas bank of the Rio Grande. Ranged out behind them were the wagonloads of contraband that were to be convoyed duty-free into Mexico — a first night's shipment of more than seventy-five thousand dollars in cotton and tools. The flatboats were in the water, the ramps were being laid for boarding, and in a matter of minutes the initial crossing would be attempted.

"Looks quiet enough over in the State of Tamaulipas," Buchanan commented.

"Too damn quiet!" Red Leech bawled.

"Won't be for long, you yellin' like that," Buchanan said.

"You got some objection, brother?"

"He was only fooling," Lash Wall put in quickly.

"He better be!" Leech said. "And he better remember who's runnin' this shebang!"

"Wouldn't want to be accused of it myself," Buchanan said.

"What?" Leech demanded.

"Where the hell's your patrol?" Buchanan

demanded right back. "Ought to've had men over there for the past two nights, getting the lay of the land, giving you some idea of what to expect when those flatboats get across."

"Don't you tell me my goddamn business!" Leech thundered. "I been fightin' the Mex for five years and never been licked yet!"

"Not at shoutin', anyhow," Buchanan said.

"What'd you say?"

Buchanan looked past him to Lash Wall. "All the same to you," he said, "I think I'll swim across and have a look-see."

"Good idea. I'll go with you."

"We'll all go!" Leech ordered. "Follow me!" He put his horse down the bank and into the river. Buchanan and Wall trailed along behind, not so noisily, and they both wished that the red-headed man wouldn't urge his mount toward the other side at the top of his voice. "Get up there!" he shouted. "Swim, you four-legged bastard!"

The far bank suddenly blazed with rifle fire.

It was a detachment under the command of Sgt. Miguel Gomez, one of the thirty strung out along the river between the bridges at Matamoros and Rio Rico. General Antonio Cueva, commander-in-chief of the Army of Tamaulipas, had known for weeks that the gringos were preparing to smuggle goods past his lucrative customs. But where would they try to ford the river? The treasury, fortunately, was full, and so Governor Diaz was able to give him the three hundred extra men and horses he needed to guard the border from invasion. The General, a brave man and a good tactician, had placed his troops in the best strategic spots — and waited.

Now the waiting was over. Red Leech's raucous entry into the water had alerted the sentries. They gave the word to Sergeant Gomez, and the sergeant ordered the open-fire.

"Red's hit!" Lash Wall yelled and he and Buchanan urged their horses forward. But it was the gang leader's mount that had taken the bullet, fatally, and now Big Red was thrashing wildly in the muddy brown water.

Another volley roared at them. Twenty rifles.

"Goddamn it, I can't swim!" Red Leech bellowed furiously.

Buchanan got to him, reached down with his arm.

"Grab on!" he said. "Climb up!"

"I'm too big!" Leech shouted from the water. "I'll pull us both under!"

"Climb up!" Buchanan ordered. Leech took the outstretched hand, put his other around Buchanan's forearm. "Heave!"

Buchanan shouted and lifted the other man clear out of the water and across the horse's rump. "You on?" he asked over his shoulder.

"Be damned if I ain't, brother!"

A third volley erupted from the other bank. Buchanan was carrying the Winchester *bandido* fashion. Now he unslung the rifle from his back, levered it and pumped. Levered and pumped. Off to his right Lash Wall threw hot lead at the opposition.

"Cut this way!" Buchanan yelled to Wall. "Come on downstream!" He swung the filly left, with the current, kept up a steady oblique fire as he went. The next barrage from the Mexicans was less organized, raggedy and confused. Then guns joined the argument from the Texas side. Frank Hancock and Sherm Moore had led a dozen men into the river as soon as the trouble started, but they had to hold their fire until they were sure they weren't going to hit their own people in the darkness. Now they were sure, and they let go with a pent-up vengeance.

Buchanan and Wall worked their horses on a gradual diagonal course to the opposite bank, scrambled up onto dry land. Big Red gave Buchanan a hearty pound on the back.

"Sure obliged for the lift, brother!" he told him. "Save your bacon sometime, let me know."

"You can save this animal of mine from

goin' swayback," Buchanan said, "by bud-
dyin'-up on that stallion of Wall's."

"Sure, brother, sure!" Leech said, getting
down. "But you know somethin'? You got a
peculiar way of sayin' things. Like you still
ain't got it clear who gives the orders and
who takes 'em."

"What order you got to issue right now?"
Buchanan asked him. The sound of firing
continued upstream without letup.

"What do you mean?" Leech demanded.

"Well, here we are in Mexico. And a quar-
ter-mile away are some Mexicans. What are
you going to do about it, mister?"

"Why, I'm gonna wait till the rest of the
boys get here!" Leech shouted. "Then I'm
gonna take them Mexicans apart!"

"They'll turn tail and run on you," Buchanan said. "Then they'll hide and pester
you all night with snipefire."

"And what the hell would you do about
it?"

"Seein' as we're over here, Leech, I'd go
on back up there right now and hit 'em
from behind."

"The three of us?"

"We could sound like a lot if we kept
moving around," Buchanan said. "And who
knows? We might get you a horse for the
one you just lost."

"The boys," Lash Wall said, "might appre-
ciate a litle assist from the rear."

"Well let's don't sit here gabbin' about it!" Leech bawled, climbing up behind Wall. "Let's go!"

There was nothing lacking in the courage of Sergeant Gomez. Three factors, though, worked against him. Number one, he was never meant to command other men. His nature was too easy-going. Number two, he did not share the customs money with General Cueva and Governor Diaz. Sergeant Gomez soldiered for twenty pesos a month. Number three, as a sixteen-year-old recruit he had witnessed the charge of the First Texas Volunteers across the plain at Monterrey during the war. It had made a lasting impression.

And though this wasn't the open fields in the blaze of noon, the black banks of the Rio could be just as unsettling even to a man of courage. On top of which, what had looked to be nothing more than a three-man foray across the river had suddenly burst into a full-blown assault. The shooting, the wild shouting, the relentless advance of the crazy gringos brought back memories.

Gomez was about to give the order to retreat when he suddenly found himself surrounded. Or so it seemed, as Leech, Wall and Buchanan laid a withering fire on his flanks.

"Sargento! Sargento!" Corporal Aguirrez cried. "What do we do?"

"How do I know?" Gomez shouted back. "Do whatever you want to!"

"But you are the sergeant!"

"I resign! Aguirrez, you are the sergeant!"

"Then I surrender!" the other man said immediately. *"Basta!"* he yelled at the top of his lungs. *"Basta!"*

"Hold it," Buchanan said to Lash Wall. "Somebody's giving up."

"Givin' up?" Big Red said, disappointed. "Hell, we just got here! Gome on, let's lay it on 'em."

Buchanan reached out, tipped Leech's carbine skyward.

"Why not give 'em a break?" he suggested. "The poor bastards probably don't even know what the shootin's all about."

"They started it, didn't they? Plugged a good horse right from under me! Take your goddamn hands offen that rifle."

"Hell, Big Red," Wall the peacemaker put in, "where's the profit in shooting some soldiers? We got a big load of freight to be moved."

"You and this ranny seem to agree on most everything, don't you?" Leech demanded suspiciously.

"Big Red," Wall said, "I agree with anything that gets us closer to the end of this work and nearer the payoff."

"All right," Leech said grudgingly. "We'll let the buggers give up."

The terms of the surrender were short and sweet. Throw the guns in a pile, tether the horses, and start walking due south. Leech promised that a patrol would be sent to check them within two hours. Any stragglers would be shot.

The Mexicans buried their six dead, took off with their wounded toward Matamoros. Leech had lost one man and his horse in the half-an-hour skirmish. Word went back across the river to start moving the wagons and the smuggling was officially underway.

"That was a good stunt, Big Red," Sherm Moore told the leader while the escort waited for the flatboats.

"What was?"

"Slippin' in behind them. Man, you sure took the pressure off us boys in the water."

"The head man's supposed to do the thinkin'," Leech said, his voice low and out of Buchanan's hearing. "That's why he takes the extra cut. You didn't tote a jug across, by any chance, Sherm?"

"Hell, no, I didn't!" Moore laughed. "But I'll scout you up one. That was a real good stunt, Big Red."

The convoy was finally assembled on Mexican soil and the trek began inland toward the first of the pre-arranged rendez-vous outside San Fernidino. There a representative of the Brownsville merchants would be waiting with the Mexican buyer to check the delivery of the contraband.

And in his headquarters at Rio Rico, General Cueva was impatiently awaiting a report on what the firing was about downriver. No report came and so the general sent Captain Luis Maximo to investigate with a full company.

Maximo was the pride of the general's staff, a young man with a great career ahead of him in the military. Why, in Strategics-and-Tactics in the military academy, Maximo had scored an unprecedented one hundred per cent. He knew by heart all of Julius Caesar's campaigns in Gaul, could trace the great battles fought by Alexander, Hannibal, Napoleon. And, in a much-discussed treatise down in Mexico City, the brilliant tactician had proved on paper how Santa Ana could have defeated Zachary Taylor by simply positioning one regiment differently and making better use of his cannons and mortars. It was titled: "How I Would Have Won At Buena Vista."

Captain Maximo knew just about everything there was to know about military warfare, and if Big Red Leech had only read the same books the outcome would never have been in doubt. Unluckily for Maximo, however, the ex-U.S. Army cavalry sergeant from Missouri had never read a book about anything. Leech's strategy in a battle was to kill you before you killed him, kill you any damn way he could manage it and no holds barred.

The two forces made their first contact about midnight, somewhere north of San Fernidino. A Mexican patrol led by Sergeant Esteban Zapata, sighted the convoy and reported immediately to Captain Maximo. Zapata was three-quarters Indian, also unschooled and uninterested in the science of maneuvers. He merely reported what he had observed on the trail — some fifty-odd wagons in a train that was escorted by an armed guard spread out haphazardly every thirty or forty yards on either side.

Also, Zapata reported, there was a huge man with a voice that boomed like a cannon and he seemed to be in charge. Moreover, the armed escort seemed to be well supplied with liquor.

The *capitan* smiled. This was going to be nothing more than a simple textbook problem, something the Romans had devised against Hannibal two thousand years ago; *The enemy's convoy should be approached as individual units and destroyed piecemeal, attacking the rear units first and working forward, causing great consternation in*

209

*the mind of the enemy's commander be-
cause he is naturally loath to leave his
forward units unguarded in the event of a
secondary attack there.*

A simple problem, Maximo decided, and
issued the proper orders to his three pla-
toon leaders. The company, half mounted,
half on foot, went forward with confidence
in their commander.

Except that Sergeant Zapata's reconnais-
sance patrol had itself been spotted by
three of Leech's outriders and their pres-
ence in the neighborhood relayed to Big
Red.

"Ride up the line, Hancock!" he ordered.
"Pull the boys back here!" He spoke without
a moment's consternation, no worry at all
about leaving his forward wagons exposed.
"I know them backbiters," he said to Buchanan. "Try to take us tail-end first."

"More'n likely," Buchanan agreed.

"Well, say now! Don't tell me I'm actually
doin' somethin' you ain't got no goddamn
complaints about?"

"Still don't know what you find to holler
about so much," Buchanan told him. "I ain't
in the next county, you know."

He was grinning across his saddle as he
spoke, but the other big man couldn't tell
that in the darkness.

"By Jesus," Leech thundered, "come down
offen that horse and let's settle this thing

once and for all! I don't take sass from nobody!"

"You're goin' to take a Mex slug in the seat of your britches," Buchanan told him mildly, "unless you attend to business."

"Come on, Big Red," the ever-present Lash Wall said, "let's get back there in case any trouble pops."

"It's comin', bucko!" Leech told Buchanan. "You and me are gonna tangle!" He looked around at the gathering forms of his gunfighters. "Company expected down the line!" he told them. "Spread yourselves, but don't let a goddamn thing through!"

They didn't. Captain Maximo led his column toward the wagon train expecting to find two, possibly three men riding rear point. Led the company with the bland assurance that he was the attacker, that he had the advantage of surprise. All at once he found himself in the middle of hell's hottest acre, overwhelmed by gunfire from everywhere at once, and the oddest thing about it was that in the first few seconds of the unorthodox assault, Luis Maximo truly became a soldier. Even as he was driven from the saddle with a shoulder wound his mind was clearly and coldly rejecting everything he had ever read or been taught on the subject of war and battle. And that paper he'd written on Buena Vista. These gringos had changed things completely.

The captain went down and his company was routed, one hundred and twenty men thoroughly drubbed by thirty. Some got away in the night, some picked up permanent mementos of the fight, the rest just gave up. Buchanan, who had marked Maximo heading the column and winged him, now brought the officer to Big Red Leech. Maximo, who was considered a tall Mexican, looked from one of his captors to the other and felt that he must be standing in a deep hole.

"How many boys you got along the border, anyhow?" Leech demanded.

"I am not required," Maximo answered stiffly, "to give you any information." Leech stared down as if he had come across a puzzling bug.

"And I ain't required to waste time!" he shouted, turning to Sherm Moore. "Sherm, take this jimdandy and turn him into a good injun, will you?"

"Sure will," Moore said taking Maximo in one hand, unholstering his .45 and hammering it back with the other. "Walk over here a ways, general," he told him persuasively.

"Wait!" Maximo protested, almost in disbelief. "I am a prisoner of war! You are not permitted to shoot me."

"Hell, mister, this ain't war!" Leech

roared. "This is strictly business! Go on, Sherm."

Buchanan leaned close to Maximo's ear. "Better speak your piece," he advised. "The man ain't foolin'."

"*Que diablos!*" the captain muttered, shaken.

"Come on, brother, come on!" Leech insisted. "How many in your army and where they posted?"

Luis Maximo named numbers and places. Lash Wall copied them down, fired an occasional question as a test for the truth. The answers were the same as the original statement.

"Well, this is going to help," Wall said happily. "We can raise hell where they are and slip across where they ain't. Ought to save us a good week's work."

"That's for me, brother!" Big Red said. "All right, Sherm, go shoot him!"

"Hold it, hold it," Buchanan put in, a little wearily. "A deal's a deal, Leech."

"What deal?"

"He traded you information, that's what deal."

"So now I just send him back to headquarters, that what you're sayin'?"

"Pack him along with us," Buchanan said. "When we get back across the river, lock him up till the job's done."

"The hell with that! Sherm . . ."

"I thought it was a deal, too, Big Red," Moore said.

"I guess we all did," Lash Wall added.

"Say, what's goin' on in this outfit, anyhow?" Leech demanded hotly. "Am I runnin' things, by damn, or ain't I? And if I ain't, then let's see the boyo who thinks he can walk in my boots!"

"Sure, you're running the show, Big Red," Wall assured him. "But you've also got a rep for the fair and square."

Leech looked at his lieutenant for a long moment. "And you all figure I made a deal with the Mex here?" he asked.

"That's how it seemed, Big Red."

"All right!" the red-haired giant conceded. "Pack the scudder onto a wagon and let's roll!" He mounted to his saddle. "But I'm puttin' out a warnin'!" he said then. "This is the last vote that goes agin me! The last one!" He raised his great fist. "Next time you can disagree with this!" and it looked very much like he shook it at Buchanan.

It was just a dull ride after that to San Bernadino, over to Linares, down as far south as Ciudad Victoria. Both the waiting Americans and their Mexican customers were overjoyed to see them arrive and quickly unload the goods. The Mexicans, for their part, were getting nearly twice as much cotton for the same money. The

Americans were doubling their profits. It was, undoubtedly, a good deal for everyone but the Governor of the State and his cronies.

Lash Wall was all for turning the empty train around pronto and going back across the river for the next load. Big Red, spying a cantina still open for business at two o'clock in the morning, overruled him.

"We earned some money tonight!" he said boisterously. "Now let's spend a little of it!" So in they went to the oasis, startling the half a dozen natives who were practically asleep in the place. Leech led the way to the bar with a clomp of bootheels that set the overhead chandelier swaying perilously.

"Set 'em up, amigo!" he told the old bartender. "Just put the bottles out and we'll do the honors!"

"*Yo no sabe, señor,*" the ancient said, shaking his head at Leech and the whole hard-bitten crew. "*No sabe ingles.*"

"Whisky!" Leech bawled at him, and then a female voice spoke.

"*Licor por los hombres,*" she translated. "*Las botellas.*" A black-haired, black-eyed girl in a short skirt and cotton blouse, she walked into the center of the room with a saucy swing of her torso.

Big Red slapped his palms together, beamed down at her like an expectant wolf.

"Well, come over here!" he said juicily. "Ain't you a flower in the desert!" She came right to him, smiling.

"For the wheesky," she said. "You got the dinero, no?"

"Hell, yes, I got dinero," Leech said. "Whatta you take me for, a deadbeat? Lash, put some money on the bar!"

Wall reached into his moneybelt, dug out two ten-dollar coins and laid them down. The girl scooped them up, bit them hard between her gleaming little teeth, smiled again and handed them to her grandfather.

Big Red roared his enjoyment at her distrust, uncorked a bottle of the Taos lightning and handed it to the lady. She shook her head.

"How much you pay," she asked him, "eef I show you dance?"

Leech roared again. "Depends how much you gonna show!" he told her and the rest of the gang laughed with him. Even Buchanan, who lifted a second bottle and a glass from the bar, turned and walked with it to a quiet table in a dark corner.

The girl raised the skirt above her shapely knee. "I dance *flamenco*," she said tauntingly. "How much you pay?"

Big Red reached down to raise the hem of the skirt higher. She jumped nimbly out of the way.

"You pay," she told him, "then you see."

"What?" Leech said. "*Me,* buy a pig in a poke?" His voice was a bellow of good humor.

The girl shrugged. "Then you no see," she said and abruptly turned away, started for the door.

"Hey, come on back here!" Leech ordered. "Let's see that dance of yours."

She stopped, looked back over her shoulder. "How much?"

"Five dollars!" he told her. "But it better be worth it!"

"Ten," she said.

"For a *dance?*"

"The *flamenco,*" she said.

"I'll chip in a dollar," Frank Hancock said. "Whatever the hell a *flamenco* is."

"Me, too," another gunman said. "Sounds special."

Leech raised his hand and scowled at them. "This is my party and I'm payin'," he said. "Lash, hand over another coin." Wall sighed, but did as Leech said. The girl took the gold and dropped it into the neck of her blouse. She went around behind the bar, then, came back with a castanet and a tambourine, moved to the center of the dimly lighted wooden floor and kicked off her flat-soled shoes. A silence fell over the place as she stood there with the castanet held above her head, body poised and erect.

The castanet clicked, clicked again, began

a smooth, rhythmic rattling. Her bare shoulders moved, then her breasts and her slim hips. She raised up on the tips of her toes and gave the tambourine a staccato *whap!* That began the dance. She glided sideways, as if on air, moved back again, came toward Leech provocatively, retreated when he made a playful grab for her. She did that one more time then pirouetted. The skirt ballooned outward, showed enough of her legs in a brief instant to whet Big Red's appetite for more. Now she increased the tempo with the castanet, struck the tambourine on her elbow, her knees, her backside, began writhing and wiggling her body in wild abandon.

Not so wild, though, that she didn't manage to keep out of Big Red's reach. She spun away from him, skirt flying above her thighs, and Leech began to stalk her around the room, grinning wickedly and egged on by his gang at the bar. The dancer whirled around faster and faster, her figure almost a blur in the dimness, and Leech closed in.

The dance, or whatever it was, came to an abrupt end when the girl spun herself down into Buchanan's big lap, threw her arms around his neck in friendly fashion.

"Hola, guapo!" she told him.

"Hello, yourself," he said.

"You take care of Rita, no?"

"Well . . ." He raised his glance to the hovering figure of Big Red Leech.

"Hand her over, brother!" Leech demanded.

"No, no!" Rita answered. "Dance ees over. I'm weeth heem now."

"Like hell you are!" Leech reached down for her and she put a bare foot in the center of his belly, pushed hard.

"Dance ees over!" she yelled sharply. "Go way now!"

Buchanan, the innocent bystander, took a casual pull at his glass of whisky.

"I'm gettin' more'n that for ten dollars!" Big Red stormed down at the girl in his lap. "Leggo that wench, bucko!"

Buchanan showed him the drink in one hand, the other holding nothing. The girl settled closer against him, tightened her grip around his neck.

Leech, infuriated, took a swipe at the glass. The whisky splashed into Buchanan's face and the glass went flying across the room. Leech bent down quickly, wrapped his hands around the front legs of the chair and upended it. Buchanan went over onto the back of his head and the screaming Rita with him. He lay there for another moment gazing quietly upward at the fiercely grinning redheaded man.

"Move out of the way," he told the girl and she rolled to one side, scampered to her feet. Buchanan rolled the other way, made the mistake of taking his eyes off Leech. Big Red's size-14 boot caught him behind the ear, flattened him out on his face this time. Buchanan lay still again, silently bawling himself out for his carelessness, feeling the thirst for battle rise sweet and warm through his chest.

Leech was laughing down at him, mockingly. Buchanan, with his back to the standing man, began to rise a second time, very slowly. Suddenly he dropped back down. Leech's boot grazed the top of his head, and as it went by Buchanan grabbed it and shoved.

Leech came down and Buchanan got up. Big Red, half-strangling on his rage, started to rise again immediately. Buchanan waited patiently, then drove his fist into the middle of those red whiskers. And stared respectfully. For all Leech did was shake his head to clear it and come wading on in. Buchanan took careful aim, cocked his fist and threw it against Leech's broad nose. The bridge made a loud popping noise but Big Red's forward momentum was unchecked. Buchanan tried him down below, buried his left fist to the wrist in Leech's belly. The man grunted and laid a sledgehammer along Buchanan's jaw. His other hand got into Buchanan's thick hair, gripped it tight and yanked hard. Buchanan's lip slammed against the top of Leech's bowed head. White lights dazzled his brain and his knees buckled. Knees. He brought the right one up, drove it home, and Leech abruptly let go of his hair and quit using him for a battering ram.

The two men stood back from each other, as if by some signal, and filled their lungs with air. Then Leech jammed his boot down onto Buchanan's instep, brought up an uppercut that was intended to stretch Buchanan's neck, followed with a round-house left to the ear that started bells ringing. Buchanan didn't pause to listen to them, punched a straight, shoulder-pow-ered right into the red blob that was Leech's freely bleeding nose. Did it again and Big Red gave ground. Buchanan jolted him a third time with a chopping left that set up the bewhiskered jaw for the hardest punch the west Texan had ever thrown in his life.

Leech took it, stood there with his arms at his side, swaying back and forth and smiling foolishly through his split lips and broken teeth. Buchanan reached out, put his hand on the redhead's great chest and pushed gently. Leech went down with a crash that knocked the bottle from the table. Buchanan retrieved it, hoisted it by the neck and let it pour for a full and wonderful five seconds.

They came away from the bar, their voices

hushed, their faces reverent, and stood looking down at Big Red as if this was his wake. Lash Wall broke the silence.

"Well, Buchanan, you did it," he said. "And even though I see him there I don't believe it." There was deep regret in the man's voice, the sorrow they all felt for a fallen champion.

Including the weary, battered, blood-smeared victor, who wouldn't know until the aching began that his own nose was broken again and the three knuckles on his left hand dislocated.

From the floor came a growling sound as consciousness flowed back into that massive figure. Big Red opened his eyes, stared all around, settled his gaze on Buchanan's face.

"You're boss now," he said solemnly. Buchanan reached down with his hand.

"Grab hold," he said. Leech took the grip and Buchanan lifted him to his feet again. Their hands stayed locked, by mutual consent.

"I got one favor to ask," Buchanan said.

"What's that?"

"Don't ask for a rematch."

Leech tried to grin. "Might lick ya, next time."

"No mights about it, Big Red. You're the bossman here."

"Well," Leech said, "at least I got my ten

dollars worth of *somethin'!*"

That reminded them both of the bone they'd been fighting over and they looked around the barroom. But the dancing girl had departed into the night, fled with her ten-dollar gold piece at that point in the battle royal when Buchanan seemed to be the certain loser.

The two big men looked for the girl then looked at each other, broke into grins that were really laughs on themselves. Buchanan wiped the top of his bottle with his grimy shirtsleeve, extended it to Leech.

"Have a drink, Big Red," he invited.

"Well, thanks, brother! Thanks! Don't mind if I do!"

That was the start of a beautiful friendship, and along about dawn Lash Wall deposited both happy behemoths into the rear of an empty freight wagon and carted them back across the Rio again. The next night another shipment of duty-free cotton made its way into Mexico, from a point ten miles downriver, and another and another for thirteen consecutive nights.

When it could find the smugglers during the first week, the Army of Tamaulipas offered resistance. But each time it did try to interfere with the convoy the result was the same — a sorry drubbing — and the commanders in the field finally decided that non-interference with the damned gringos was the better part of valor. General Cueva resigned his commission, went back to raising horses, and Governor Diaz set up a conference with the Brownsville merchants to arrange for a reasonable ten per cent tariff on the goods shipped into Matamoros.

Everybody was happy, especially Rita in Ciudad Victoria. Rita and Linda and Josephine and Marie and Lolita — and all the girls who were waiting and eager to provide all sorts of entertainment for the free-spending Americans when each night's work was done.

Then the last shipment was delivered, the job was done, Big Red Leech threw a fine blowout that lasted three days and three nights, and his army dispersed to the four winds.

TWELVE

"BUCHANAN!"
It was a female voice that hailed him as he rode through the main drag of Brownsville, happy-sounding and vaguely familiar. He turned his head to see Cristy Ford waving to him from the seat of a shiny new brougham that was parked before the entrance to the Crystal Palace. He swung his white stallion toward the carriage, spotted John Lime exiting the casino at the same moment. The man's arm was still in a sling from the battle at the jail.

"Hello, Cristy," Buchanan greeted her. "Howdy, Sheriff."

"Well just look at you!" she exclaimed, taking in the fancy new clothes, the new boots, the clean white shirt and string tie. "Why," she said, "that's even a new horse."

"That filly fooled me," Buchanan said. "Some little runt of a mustang made eyes at her over in Nuevo Leon and she decided to become a mare."

"Heard it was a very prosperous operation," Lime said. "For all concerned."

"Not bad," Buchanan conceded. On his

broad face was the grin of content that came from the satisfying action of the past three weeks.

"We heard about all the fighting," Cristy said. "This town hasn't been talking about anything else, in fact."

"And your private fight with Leech," Lime said. "We heard about that, too."

"Things get blown up," Buchanan said. Then he stared at something that seemed to interest him more. It was the huge diamond ring that sparkled on Cristy's finger.

"Mrs. Lime?" he asked.

She nodded. "As of two weeks yesterday."

"Well, say, that's fine! Congratulations, Sheriff."

"Former sheriff," Lime told him, pulling back his jacket to show the absence of the little gold star that had been almost a part of the man. "My bride has a strong aversion to guns and gunplay," he added. "We're leaving this frontier country for the more civilized life in Virginia."

"Wish you best of luck," Buchanan said sincerely.

"Thank you. The office of Sheriff, incidentally, is up for election. Why don't you enter your name in the lists?"

"Not me," Buchanan grinned. "But I think my buddy Lash Wall will be interested."

"An outlaw?"

"Wouldn't be the first time, Mr. Lime. And

I think Lash and Brownsville deserve each other." He tipped his hat. "Well," he said, "I got to be moseyin'. Things to do."

"Where you bound for, Tom?" Cristy asked him.

"Same place," Buchanan said doggedly. "New Orleans. This time I got passage all booked. Going there by boat."

The pretty bride laughed up at him. "That," she said, "ought to be something to see!"

Buchanan bade the newlyweds good-by and good luck, rode on until he came to the Wells Fargo office. There he made three consignments of cash, two to San Antonio, the third to Jess Bogan in Alpine. The sender of the money was listed in each case as *The Double-B Fast Freight Company, R. Bogan, Prop.*

And that was the end of it.

William R. Cox was born in Peapack, New Jersey. His early career was in newspaper journalism. In the late 1930s he began writing sports, crime, and adventure stories for the magazine market, and he made his debut as a Western writer with "Night of the Blood Bucket Raid" in *Dime Western* in the January, 1941 issue. It is worth noting that his Western story debut was with the first of several stories to feature a series character, Terry Glenn. During the 1940s Cox created a number of other series characters for the magazine market, most notably the Whistler Kid who appeared regularly in *10 Story Western* and Duke Bagley whose adventures usually were featured in *Star Western*. "The short story form was blissful until there were no markets," he once recalled. In the 1950s and 1960s Cox turned to television and wrote at least a hundred teleplays for such series as "Broken Arrow," "Dick Powell's Zane Grey Theatre," "The Virginian," and "Bonanza." He also won a host of readers writing original paperback Western novels, the best known of which are novels about the adventures of two series characters originally published by Fawcett Gold Medal: Cemetery Jones in a series published under his own byline and the Tom Buchanan series which appeared under the house name, Jonas Ward. Dale L. Walker in the second edition of TWENTIETH CENTURY WESTERN WRITERS commented that William R. Cox's Western "novels are noted for their 'pageturner' pace, realistic dialogue, and frequent Colt-and-Winchester gun play. The series of novels built around the strong West Texas character, Tom Buchanan, are very typical Cox Westerns."